WHAT HAPPENED HERE

What Happened Here

a novella and stories by

Bonnie ZoBell

Press 53

Winston-Salem

Press 53, LLC
PO Box 30314
Winston-Salem, NC 27130

First Edition

Cover design by Kevin Morgan Watson

Cover art, "Red Bird," Copyright © 2013
by Sandy Tweed, used by permission of the artist.

Author photo by Photo by Elsa
www.photobyelsa.com

Printed on acid-free paper
ISBN 978-1-941209-00-4

For Jimmy
&
for my family:
Janet, Karl, Barbara, David, Jean, Betsy, Karen, Claude, Mary, Bruce, and Helene

What Happened Here

Acknowledgments

The following stories have been published in slightly different form by the magazines listed:

"Uncle Rempt" in *Storyglossia*, nominated for Million Writers Award

"People Scream" in *Gulf Stream Magazine*, reprinted online at *Static Movement*

"Sea Life" in *Night Train*

"This Time of Night" in *American Fiction: The Best Unpublished Short Stories by Emerging Writers*, edited by Joyce Carol Oates; author received a National Endowment of the Arts Fellowship based on this story

"Dear Sam," in *Temenos*

"Nimbus Cumulus" in *The Cimarron Review*

"Movement in the Wire" in *Juked, Ascent Aspirations Borderlines Anthology*, and *Outlaws: Bannock Street Books Anthology*

"A Black Sea" in *New Plains Review*

"Rocks" in *The Los Angeles Review*, nominated for a Pushcart Prize

"Lucinda's Song" in *Prick of the Spindle*

What Happened Here

I knew all about the crash when I moved onto Boundary Street in 2003. Everyone in San Diego did. Twenty-five years earlier, the deadliest airline disaster in U.S. history occurred above our homes before we lived here. It's still the deadliest in California. PSA Flight 182 and a Cessna collided mid-air over our North Park neighborhood.

The perspective from the ground was shown afterward on the cover of *TIME* Magazine and newspapers around the world: The flaming Pacific Southwest Airlines jet carrying a hundred and thirty-seven passengers plunged towards what was now our backyards. A few neighbors who happened to look up when they heard a loud crunching sound saw the out-of-control jet careening to the right, fire and smoke shooting out from behind before the plane slammed into the earth at 300 miles per hour just behind my house. The explosion was instantaneous—an enormous fireball whooshed into the sky, a mushroom of smoke and debris. Scraps of clothing leaped onto telephone poles, body parts fell on roofs, tray tables scattered across driveways. Airplane seats landed on front lawns, arms and legs descended onto patios, and a torso fell through the windshield of a moving vehicle. While eerie, hot Santa Ana winds reportedly shot through the streets—the kind that make your hair crackle, your skin flake, your sinuses burn—metal pierced homes, chimneys, and people. The telephone pole on the corner of Dwight and Nile, jolted from the cement by the violent impact, still leans today. Twenty-two homes gone in a flash. Passengers and people, in their homes and on the street, dead.

The accident was posed to me as a ghoulish fringe benefit by the previous owner of my house. I'd be able to say I resided in a place where the tragedy had occurred. I did my part to maintain the lore, relaying details I'd read online to curious visitors. Near downtown San Diego, North Park was a place I loved from the start. I fit in better than anywhere I'd ever lived—plain folk mixed with artistic types, working and middle class residing side by side, all colors and ages, gay and straight. Lanky palm trees towered above sidewalks, gardens brimmed with magenta geraniums, red bougainvillea spilled over old fences, the odd varieties of Dr. Seussian succulents stuck their tongues out across yards. I could be anyone I wanted and still be accepted, not like the house I'd grown up in.

"We got some neighborhood macaws who're real characters," the previous owner told me. "Some say they're pretty and I suppose they are, all up in the palms. They make too much racket for my tastes, though, and leave huge macaw shit all over the place."

I worried about how the annihilation of these bodies that landed on my property would affect me. Would I feel engulfed by doom simply living on this patch of earth? I'd had bouts of depression. I didn't need to think about dead families sprawled on my back patio, even if it had been decades. But while I'd never be cured of this incessant disease, my own particular strain had been restrained after too many years of therapy and a lifetime commitment to antidepressants. My husband's had not.

I met John, a tall man with magnificent broad shoulders that made me feel more petite than I was, three years after moving to North Park. He was playing piano in a popular local band at the Waterfront, San Diego's best dive bar. I was twenty-eight, he two years older and so attractive he was embarrassing to look at— heavy eyebrows, eyes that saw through everything, a large mouth he'd been teased about in middle school but that nobody teased him about anymore. People hovered, drawn to him. A lot of the people were women. I was attracted to the light of his mania, though I didn't know it at the time. When he teased out those keys, everything from boogie woogie to slow-rolling blues emerged. His eyes closed when he sang, his voice warm and husky, and he went somewhere fervid inside, somewhere that hurt, a place where his contorted expression could have meant pure euphoria, pure anguish, or both.

I'd recently gotten out of a rotten marriage. It had taken me less than a year to discover my husband was every bit as controlling as my father.

John dropped into a seat at my table the third time I went to hear his band.

"What's your name?" he said, teetering dangerously far back on the legs of his chair.

I burned everywhere. "Lenora."

He picked up my hand, drew a line with his finger up and down my digits. "What do you do, Lenora?" He gazed at me slowly from my feet all the way up to my face in a way I'd been taught was rude, but it felt okay coming from him.

"I'm a continuing ed teacher."

He grabbed my swinging foot under the table, let the shoe drop, rubbed the ball of my heel in slow movements, the kind that work muscles in an exhilarating mixture of pleasure and pain. I considered asking him to stop, but it felt too good.

"I work for the local paper during the week," he said.

I nodded.

A strange expression materialized on his face, before he said, "And the only word there spoken was the whispered word, 'Lenore!'"

That sewed everything up right there.

"Merely this and nothing more," I replied, smiling back. I glanced down at his hand. "Is that a wedding ring?"

He let go of my foot and a faraway expression swept his face. "It's complicated," he said.

"Seems like a yes or no question."

"Don't go away."

We kept flirting until his next break, though I had a pit in my stomach.

"Where do you live?" he asked, sitting again.

"Boundary Street. North Park."

"Great old houses over there. Isn't that where the jet crashed, 1978?"

I nodded.

"My Uncle Oba's fighter plane went down in Vietnam. Crashes remind me of him."

I told him on his next break, "I don't need to get in the middle of someone else's crappy marriage." I packed up my purse.

"Don't go," he said, the front legs on his chair falling back to earth.

Grabbing my jacket, I steered myself toward the front entry, but he was right behind me as I pushed through the glass door. The sea breeze smelled fresh and briny.

I shot to my car, beeped to unlock, turned to say goodbye. His face was right there.

"Leslie and I are over," he said. "It's just I love my daughter so much."

"Oh, god, you have a daughter, too?"

"I do, a daughter I love. Abby."

I plunged into the front seat. His forearm leaned against the roof, framing his broody face. My car should already have been in gear; I should have been pulling onto the freeway by now.

My fingers pushed the hair on his forehead so far back into the massive waves on his head they seemed lost for good. "I don't want to get hurt. I don't need this. I . . ."

And then his knees sank to the sidewalk, and his mouth was on mine.

I stayed away a month. If we continued, the same thing would happen to Abby that had to me—daddy gone one morning for another woman, girl left with a tormented mom. But I was full of unrepentant pheromones with my new-found freedom. When I returned to the Waterfront, we kept our distance the first few times. Then one night we didn't. We made eyes while he was on stage. I accepted some man's offer to dance and then shimmied right in front of John. The second song in, he did a solo, an old Jeff Buckley version of "Hallelujah."

During my absence, he'd been made local editor. "No one can believe I did it at thirty-one years old," he told me. A flash of importance spread over his face. It looked good there.

He turned his phone on, took a series of incoming calls from the paper, then apologized, and powered down.

Despite the showing off, I admired his mind at work, a complex swarm of genius, a beehive of information as he rapidly worked his cell, talking story angles, problems with sources.

We ordered red beers and were speaking loudly over the din, when he leaned over and said, "You must have missed me, huh?" winking.

Our table suddenly became quiet. He kicked his foot. The despair on his face when he picked the label off his Dos Equis helped me understand he still wrote music that hurt.

We made love and were together often during the next months. Sometimes he cried about Abby. His moods changed rapidly, but his having so many emotions was exciting after growing up with a father who seemed to have none. Maybe my own father wouldn't have become so depressed if he'd left when he first grew unhappy. As it was, he was so dissatisfied with so much of his life, including me, that I turned into a girl who could never do anything right, who'd never be pretty enough, who had no sense of humor about jokes at my expense. My mother's cocktails helped her pretend. Occasionally, I still felt like that girl—stupid, ugly, and fat, isolated, because who would want me?

When I told John about this one night at dinner, he said, "Lenora, those things aren't true. You can't listen to him." Then he leaned over and kissed me.

John never knew when he could get away, but when he could,

he came to me. I'd glance out my front window, and there he'd be. I was always glad to see him. I learned all about his breakdown when he was nineteen, the months he spent in the hospital, the diagnosis of bipolar. I learned about his mother committing suicide when he was fourteen. None of this made me want him less. His father had forbidden him from revealing to anyone his hospitalization or the way his mother died. I was the first person he told.

Leslie caught him emailing me one night. She howled that he had to stop, that he couldn't see me anymore. The second time, she screeched, "Then if she's your soul mate, she can have you! Get out!" He got his own apartment for six months, then moved in with me. Leslie and Abby were heartbroken. John saw his daughter every chance he got, agonized when he couldn't. I didn't go with him since I knew she really wanted to see him, not me, as I had only wanted to see my father, not my stepmother, Philomena. John grew quieter and darker. What would I have thought if it had been easy for him to leave?

Murmurings about the upcoming commemoration of PSA Flight 182 started in the summer of 2007. Would the city finally put up a memorial on the corner behind our house where the airplane hit? There was a plaque in the San Diego Aerospace Museum, and on the 20th anniversary, a tree was planted in front of the North Park library with another plaque. Neither was close to the site, though. Maybe even thirty years later it was still too raw a reminder of what happened here for folks going about their daily basis.

The first we heard of our next-door neighbor, Archie, planning a neighborhood block party as a thirty-year remembrance of the crash was that November. Nobody worked the story of PSA 182 as hard as Archie. Tall and stringy, he came running over one afternoon with a worn manila folder just as we were getting in the car. Every chance he got, Archie explained to me even more specifically than the previous owner exactly where the plane had crashed—over our fences on Boundary Street—and in even greater detail how our homes had been affected. A statistician for the federal government, he wore his tangerine-colored hair pulled into a neat ponytail at the nape of his neck. Before we could even say hello, he spotted our garden hose, uncoiled and flopped across the garden.

"Hoses wrapped up neatly in the holder make the whole neighborhood look better," he said, catching his breath.

"I'm going to garden more this afternoon," I told him.

I rolled my eyes at John when Archie wasn't looking. John shrugged. He'd become more tolerant of Archie since he'd found out that he, too, suffered his own brand of hopelessness. About the only thing we had in common, besides living next door and owning houses that were the resting place for a lot of ghosts, was that both men had had recent run-ins with the black monster, who snuck up and took over when they weren't looking.

"Anybody with the problem is a brother," John told me. "Archie's a brother and that guy with a bum leg on the corner. The receptionist at the newspaper's a sister."

John's father had tried to beat from him any natural acceptance of a different life, including the sin of playing his guitar instead of constantly practicing to be the town's star quarterback. Our neighbor being so unswervingly out was something new for him.

Archie'd had a serious boyfriend, but I hadn't noticed the guy's SUV lately. Instead, I saw a lone Archie wandering the neighborhood more frequently, knocking on doors.

Above us that day on the driveway, a flurry of color—scarlet, turquoise, mustard—zipped past, shrieking and hustling, from one North Park palm tree to another. The brilliance of these neighborhood macaws flying through our Southern California enclave in formation, twenty-five of them together to forage for dates, could allow just about anyone to forget the rest of the world. Escapees from unlatched cages all over town, not to mention the zoo, they'd fled front doors left open only for a minute, chewed through screens when left alone too long, and now banded together to make North Park their home.

"Wow," John said as he and I stared so as not to miss any of the colorful show.

"Amazing." I was enthralled. "Diving out of the sky with all those intense colors."

"Cool!" Heather called from her apartment balcony next door, still in her pajamas. Her boyfriend wore a dog collar and waved.

The five of us crinked our necks upward to watch the macaws until they'd all flown by.

Shaking his head at the noisy birds, Archie opened his folder. "Look what I found at the public library," he said, pulling out copy after copy of aerial views of the airline crash.

"See right there?" Bending ninety-degrees beside my window, he pointed at a photo with our house in it. "Right by the carport?" he continued. "The people before you tore that down. See the crater on your lawn? Who knows what landed there? See?" He pointed to a spot in our yard.

John, startled, dropped the car keys on the floor mat. He seemed unable to look away from our home's scar.

"September 25th, 2008, everyone can come to my place for the anniversary," Archie said. "We'll appease the gods so it'll never happen again."

Archie took off, and we sat there. "Time to go, John," I said.

"John?" I repeated.

Finally he snapped out of it, but then we switched places so he wouldn't have to drive.

Who knows why that particular day was so hard when he already knew about the crash? Maybe it was because he now lived on the property, making him a part of it.

"Did I ever tell you about my Uncle Oba? The one who was in Vietnam and . . ."

"Yep. You have."

My father, too, was a brother. In the seventies, he'd had Elavil and Librium.

Weeks later when I called my dad, he said, "You mother says this John's still married." We rarely spoke. Email was far safer so I didn't have to worry about his mood when he received it. I liked to think I'd gotten over him years ago, but talking to the man could still hurt.

"You mean like you were married when you met Philomena? I thought you'd want to meet him. Anyway, the divorce papers have all been filed."

"He has problems with depression?"

"Sounds familiar, doesn't it?" I said.

"No reason to go looking for people like that."

I took a few deep breaths. "Maybe I wouldn't be attracted to people with such highs and lows if you'd shown any emotion at all or talked to me about things that mattered."

The following silence was riotous.

"Give me a call when he's your husband," he said.

John didn't go down right away. Just the opposite.

A few months after moving in, we went out with Alexa, a Greek painter I'd met down the street. Her husband Eduardo had to work late.

"Is that a mustache?" John asked Alexa in the loud restaurant. A piano player chinked out music on the other side of the partition, and customers took turns singing with him.

"*John!*" I said.

"What?" Eyes twinkling, he seemed pleased with himself. "Just stating the obvious."

"Why would you say something like that?" I asked him.

Alexa seemed unsure, but laughed. "That's okay. I can take it. Me and Frida Kahlo."

Until recently, I'd never seen this new, in-your-face behavior of John's before.

Unable to sit still, he said, "I'm going to sing," and wandered off.

Soon his voice was belting out over all the others. Fortunately, it was a good voice.

He sang a passionate "I wish I was special"—"Creep," by Radiohead.

"He's good," Alexa shouted, laughing. "I wish I could get Eduardo to loosen up like that. John's so fun." She beamed towards him. "Don't you think?"

"Sure."

We left napkins over our dinners—John still hadn't touched his—and leaned into the bar clapping while John sang "Stuck on You" by Elvis.

Now he was standing on his bar stool. The bartender didn't look pleased, but everyone was buying drinks, so nobody said anything.

"Wow," Alexa said.

"I guess he's had a few."

My stomach tripped over the food I'd just eaten. When an older woman argued with John over the microphone, I stomped over and took him by the arm. "It's someone else's turn."

The elderly lady asked him to dance when the microphone moved on to someone else.

Back at the table, I told him, "Alexa's got an early appointment. Aren't you tired?"

"I'll take a cab." He didn't seem to mind at all that we were leaving him behind.

"Is everything okay?" Alexa asked on the drive home.

I shrugged.

At 3:00 a.m. a policewoman dropped him off at the curb in front of our place.

I didn't know what he might do next. As this energy continued, I became increasingly sure we weren't going to make it.

I asked one morning, "Don't you think you should see a doctor, hon?" Most of our house had been redone since 1929, except for our kitchen. It wasn't quaint. It was small with broken plumbing. We bumped into each other a lot.

"I don't see why."

"Is this mania?" I waited until the microwave said my coffee was ready.

"Maybe."

"It's exhausting. Remember what your doctor said—what goes up must come down."

"I feel great. No way I'm coming down on purpose." He was off to take Abby for a haircut and then to a birthday party. Afterwards he had a tee time with a friend.

In May he became convinced he'd write a book. "Plenty of journalists write them. Who else has the discipline? I write every day for work. I write songs a lot. You like my songs."

This seemed fine until I got home one afternoon and he was at the dining table with legal pads scribbled all over. There were three half-drunk cups of coffee. I found out soon enough he was on the phone with Tim O'Brien. I was spellbound. How did someone get Tim O'Brien on the phone?

"I know," John said, "but how did you go from *The Washington Post* to writing your first novel?"

I tiptoed away, lay on the couch while they talked another half an hour. Then he called Chuck Palahniuk. I took a deep breath, worn out from the last conversation.

"You were a diesel mechanic?" John said.

Sometimes the thought of a boyfriend who liked to watch mystery movies together at night and doze off on the couch seemed tremendously appealing. How he got them to talk wasn't as confusing. At full-tilt, John was hard to resist. Had I ever been attracted to normal, breadwinning, logical men?

He called Carl Hiaasen.

A month or two later, John came home with five computers, one for him for work-related issues, one for his personal use, one for me, one for Abby, and one for guests.

"Where are we going to put them all?" I asked.

"We'll use them. You'll see."

Fortunately, just as quickly as he'd left me for some other planet in the stratosphere, he was back. For a while, he could be counted on again. My old love had returned. He reveled in salvaging egg-shaped doorknobs from architectural hardware stores to match the era of our house, built archways in our doorways to go with the Spanish mission style. It was his way, since he'd moved in after me, of owning part of what the house was all about.

I was reading on the couch one weekend, only half paying attention, when he came through and said for the first time in a long time, "And so faintly you came tapping, tapping at my chamber door." I sat up, startled, smiled. "Darkness there, and nothing more."

"Lenore, Lenore . . ." I said, laughing.

When a student was rude to me that winter, John drove the two of us to the mountains—Julian, an old mining camp—serenaded me with his harmonica. "The kid's a punk," he said, before giving me a long, burly hug, one that made me forget everything else. "He should respect you more."

Abby spent a night with us most weekends. At eight years old, she wanted to sit on her dad's lap constantly. Leslie dropped her off one evening before John got home. The dogs and cats surrounded Abby, and she sat on the hard-wood floor, giggling, let them lick her face and hair.

"Are these your children?" she asked.

"No, you're the children."

"But I'm only one."

"You're enough for all of us. We're lucky."

She stood, perched on the arm of a couch. "But you're not my mother. You and my dad aren't even married."

Carefully, I said, "No, your mother is your mother. But I like you a lot."

She stared at her hands. "Do you think my dad will be home soon?"

"Any minute."

"Can I see what's in your refrigerator?'

"Definitely."

We headed to the kitchen. When I opened the door and gazed inside, I realized all we had were Spanish olives, nonfat milk, and beer. We went out a lot. "We could make jello."

"Jello!" she said, in a voice younger than her years. Maybe she was trying too hard, too.

Twenty minutes later when John walked in, she was standing on an aerobics step, mixing in the apple we'd cut up.

"There's my girl," he said. She dropped everything, jumped off the step, and flew over to hug his legs. It made me happy to see him happy.

Occasionally he still cried about leaving her, and I felt awful. I wondered if my father had cried after he left. Maybe I just hadn't known. Maybe I should have encouraged John to go back.

But then he'd come home from another horrible fight with Leslie. "She fucking thinks I should pay even more support since you work full time, too."

Or she'd pick on him for not seeing Abby enough, but when he tried to see her extra, she complained he was trying to take her away. Leslie would shout at him, "She's all I've got!"

Towards the end of the year, the Friday after his divorce was final, we decided to drive up to Big Bear and get married.

"Are you sure?" I said.

He rested his chin on my head. "More than anything. What about you?"

"I've always wanted to marry you."

What would it have been like to marry a regular guy who wore a suit every day and expected the house to be neat? What if I'd had to go to company picnics and be polite to assholes because they were my husband's bosses or have parties with wives I had nothing in common with? I'd rather die. So, yes, John felt deeply about Abby, tended toward the melancholy and the other extreme, but he was real. He let me be me.

We drove the long way to Big Bear, up the coast, then tracked down a wedding consultant, who turned out to be new age. We wrote poems for each other. That night was one of the happiest in my life. We made love, went out to dinner, made love again.

Archie knocked in February wearing gym clothes and aviator sunglasses. "Hey, you think you could get your dogs to stop barking so much?"

"Nobody else has mentioned anything," I told him.

"They're being polite."

He'd complained about other things, Abby leaving a couple of toys on the lawn, our cat eating his feral cat's food.

"But if the cats are outside and you feed them there, I don't see what I can do," I said.

Secretly, Archie loved our cat visiting him. "You just going to sit there, girlfriend, while I scratch your head?" I overheard him telling her. He liked the dogs, too. The solution to barking? Give him a key and permission to lock them in our house if they were barking and we weren't home. After that, I saw signs of Archie visiting the animals, balls thrown across the lawn, leftover rinds from oranges he must have fed the dogs from his tree. One time when I drove up after teaching, John was inside playing "Hotel California" on the piano, and I spied Archie through the fence cooing and kissing them. It was that empty house of his, him and all those phantoms. He'd become something of a ghost himself.

When John got home a few days later, I saw the two of them talking and stepped outside. "You seem to be doing good," John was telling Archie. "Back at work and all?"

He rocked on his feet, alluding to Archie's recent hospitalization for depression. John had immediately gone to see him when we found out, but I was working. Despite the complaints, I felt for the man. We knew he wasn't HIV positive, so I wondered why he hadn't gained enough weight back after being discharged that winter and spending several weeks at home.

"I'm okay," Archie said quickly.

All of our heads rotated upward to our North Park palm fronds as macaws roughhoused with massive chatting and squawking. A fledgling pecked the beak of an older bird, who pecked back, a duel to the death, only they weren't pecking very hard. Still another dive bombed one of my cats in the side yard then swooped militia style back up to the tree, squealing in laughter, swinging upside down from a frond.

Regardless of what the talk turned to among the neighbors,

though, we rarely invited the others inside. Without an official gathering, it seemed too intimate.

By March of 2008, though there were still six months to go until the thirtieth anniversary of Flight 182 being hurled onto our street from above, our North Park neighborhood was abuzz. The owner of our corner bodega ruminated over a carton of eggs about how such a wretched accident had ever occurred. Where were the air traffic controllers? The mailwoman had been leaving for school and saw the black smoke. The SDG&E meter reader was in elementary school looking out the windows at the falling ashes. The telephone repairman saw it on the news in Washington, where he grew up.

As if calibrated by some mysterious clock, as soon as the anniversary began to be talked about, John started drinking more. He sank, slept too much, lost weight, didn't want to do anything. Now that we were married, he'd brought a dining room table from his old house, an ancient chair that rocked too far back, a framed picture of his favorite Uncle Oba sitting in the cockpit of his plane that went down in Vietnam and wearing a green Air Force jumpsuit and a helmet with an oxygen mask, his eyes smiling. The dining table stayed, the chair went, Uncle Oba watched everything we did.

John began blaming the fiery metal nightmare plummeting from the sky for causing such a ravenous reoccurrence of despair in him. He was sure there was a parallel to the anniversary.

He stopped returning phone calls.

"But Abby doesn't understand why you won't talk to her," I said.

"It's not good for her to see me like this." He bunched up under his covers, the curtains closed all weekend. He told Leslie to tell Abby he loved her, but he was sick. Sometimes when John became particularly low he disappeared on long walks. The airplane disaster carefully consigned to a back corner of my mind, I searched desperately to understand and not be so afraid when John sank even lower into the black hole.

"Is it because you're not living with Abby anymore?" I asked.

"I'm so sorry about that. Maybe I should have stayed."

"I wanted you, though."

"I know, but she's just a little girl."

Another day I said, "Maybe it's because your job's so stressful." He was on call one night a week. Something catastrophic always seemed to happen: someone broke out of the downtown jail, a child was kidnapped and driven over the Tijuana border, a whale got stuck in the bay.

"Probably," he said.

I decided there was no reason. It swooped out of nowhere like the macaws, stayed as long as it liked. Who knew how this disease decided when to descend except by alignment of some mysterious chemical tumult.

In April, Archie started talking more about the neighborhood block party for the thirtieth anniversary. I was weeding when he came by. "The whole neighborhood'll get together and remember," he said. "We'll quiet all those souls, tell them to rest so we can go on with our lives."

The neighborhood part sounded fun. "I hope everyone comes."

His mouth twitched, and he almost smiled.

Burgeoning public interest in the history of the North Park crash meant John had already been required to start assigning articles for the *Union-Tribune* to cover the disaster.

"I'm not sure I'm the best guy for the job," he said one night, the television only partially masking the slight quaver in his voice.

"Why not?"

"Well, it all happened right here . . . outside." He didn't look away from the TV.

"But nobody else seems to be getting depressed about it."

"You don't know that."

I straightened magazines in the living room. "Can't someone else be in charge of this?"

"I'm the editor. I'm the guy." He shrugged, foot kicking. "One reporter's interviewing the pilot's wife. Another's talking to survivors. A filmmaker's doing a documentary."

By May, still four months before the anniversary, John was drinking four vodka tonics every evening. If there wasn't any tonic, he just drank vodka. He still wasn't seeing Abby much. I'd grown to care about her and missed her. Leslie called to say she didn't want him around Abby if he was drinking. He cut down to three drinks every night.

He arrived home late from work one evening.

"I was worried," I told him.

"I went into all the old files at work and read every article about the crash I could get my hands on." He slumped onto the couch.

I sat next to him, as close as I could. "Why?"

"Un-fucking-believable," he added. "It was a 727 Boeing. Sixty-six tons, six tons of fuel alone, just dropped on the neighborhood. Can you believe it?" He wasn't talking to me. It was some important conversation he was having with himself. "The jet was preparing for final landing at Lindbergh Field," he continued. "The pilots never saw the Cessna. You know how hard it is to land there with all those skyscrapers hugging the runway."

He punched a fist into his hand. "One local news guy giving an on-the-scene report looks down while he's on the air and realizes he's standing on a set of somebody's teeth."

"Gross." I petted the hair on his arm.

"Uncle Oba went down just like that."

Later, lying on the backyard grass, we stared up at the sky and watched a plane head for the airport, our house only a few miles north of the flight pattern. The plane route must have moved south after the accident. A neighborhood should only have to pay once.

Despite the jet being all those miles above, it was descending, drawing closer. I could see the cabin lights on against the night sky, sense activity inside, human life.

John sat up. "Who knows what world we'll end up in when this one is over?"

A couple of straggling macaws screamed overhead, no doubt

trying to catch up with the rest of the flock so they could brood together for the night.

My father called. I imagined him sitting at his sharp-cornered desk in his office.

"Eight months," I told him, when he asked how long I'd been married.

Silence.

Long ago I'd decided he loved me because of the occasional calls and emails. To have a relationship, I had to imagine what a healthy man might feel in a given situation and attribute those emotions to him. It was tedious, but he was my father.

That day I interpreted the lull as his respecting me for not telling him I got married, for not getting emotional. Nothing makes him more uncomfortable.

Two nights later, he called to say he was parked out front and would like to come in.

"Ed Jacobson," he said inside, reaching his hand out to John.

"John," John said.

Dad stood there, unsure.

"Do you want to sit down?" I asked. That would at least take up a little time.

"For a minute."

"Do you want some orange juice? Beer?"

"Just water, thank you."

He lowered himself into an uncomfortable dining chair, which was probably the most comfortable for him. A couch would have made him sink in.

John sat as far away as possible.

"My dad wrote for his college newspaper," I said, then slipped into the kitchen. I could hear them talking, which fascinated me.

"We feel most people don't write well," my father said as I set three glasses of water before us, apparently speaking for himself and John. He wore a suit and tie, as he did every day of his life. "Of course, I write quite well."

I laughed because I knew this was meant to be a self-deprecating joke, though not a very good one because he was a good writer. Then John laughed.

"You can't expect everybody to write as well as you do," I said.

"No," Dad said, taking a sip of water.

We talked about the weather, the Padres.

"I have to go," he said, standing.

John hovered near the front door, no doubt trying to figure out what a husband meeting his wife's father for the first time should say. "Well, sir, I love your daughter, and . . ."

"Yes, it's nice to meet you," my father said, shaking hands, and then he was out the door.

In July, John came home from work early for the first time since I'd known him, went straight to bed without eating, and slept for twelve hours. I noticed he had hand tremors.

"They're from my antidepressants," he said.

"You've never had them before." In and out of doctors' offices since college, he'd long ago burned out on therapists, who seemed unable to help, though he had to go to one for meds.

Soon after, he was telling reporters they'd have to approach the North Park survivors for interviews on their own and not to ask him so many questions. Not the usual hyper John, willing to jump in and chew over any story, he turned off his cell phone.

Archie stopped by in early September to confirm the neighborhood party was on for the 25th. I stiffened in the kitchen when I saw him knocking since I wasn't in the mood for more complaints. To avoid his detection from the porch, I remained motionless while the dogs jumped and shimmied like maniacs since they'd grown fond of him.

He spoke to me right through the screen. "Are you aware you drove over the new tar the city put down?" He couldn't see me because I had a security screen, metal, the kind even a rapist can't get through.

I knew I should step outside and talk since it didn't sound like a brief complaint, but I wasn't wearing a bra, and even though he was gay, it didn't seem right. Quickly throwing one on, I cracked the screen.

"Sorry," I said. "Didn't get home until dark. The city said it would wear off in a month."

He couldn't find an agreeable spot to stand.

I pulled the door open and stood on the porch, leaning on one hip in a way that said I was committed for at least a few minutes. Then John drove up from work, a troubled crease between his brows. I wrapped my arm around his waist and squeezed.

"Hey, man," they said, shaking hands. A colorful triumvirate, we stood on the hot driveway: the redheaded Archie whose jeans had ironed creases down the front. The brown-haired John, who'd started a beard. My blond head gazing up since both were almost a foot taller.

"Well," Archie said, "I wanted to remind you about the party. It'll be an all afternoon and evening thing so people can stop by and chat whenever they like."

At the mention of Archie's party on that date we all knew about, suddenly, with no warning, John lowered himself to the sidewalk, stretched his arms straight out at the sides as if appealing to some unknown being above.

"Don't do that, John," I said, nervous. "Get up."

Archie shook his head.

At first John wouldn't move, just lay there.

"John, that's creepy," I said.

So he stood, folded his arms protectively over his thick chest. "You got to at least avoid looking at the ugly," he mumbled, "or it'll drive you crazy. All this talk about the accident. Sometimes it's better to just look at nature and not think about these things."

We glanced up, but all there was in front of us was Archie's usual landscaping feat—his shrubs mutilated into such precise boxes they no longer seemed alive.

"Ha!" Archie said, clearly unsure of what to make of any of it.

❖   ❖   ❖

North Park news via all outlets was whirring, and John's office was no exception. A memorial was planned for the morning of September the 25th at the corner of Dwight and Nile. I could see it a block away over our back fence.

"I'm not going," John said that morning. "I got a reporter assigned. I can't stand watching anymore people crying about dead family members and dead cats being found on roofs."

"You want to skip Archie's party, too?"

"Nah. Archie's a brother. He gets it."

So I hovered by the rear window that morning trying to see anything I could, which wasn't much besides the backs of people.

Late in the afternoon, we heard musicians warming up at Archie's gathering next door. Tables were being moved to the backyard since the weather was balmy. Our dogs barked a few times at the hubbub before they got used to it.

That evening, we all came out of our bungalows and converged at Archie's party. There were no Santa Ana winds like that night thirty years earlier, but there was an eeriness. Supposedly Archie's party wasn't arranged solely because of the PSA crash but because we who lived on the site rarely had time to socialize except to nod while deadheading our snapdragons.

We advanced onto Archie's front lawn at the same time as Alexa, my painter friend from down the street, and her husband, Eduardo. Alexa and I hugged.

"Hope you'll do some singing tonight, John," Alexa said, winking.

John shook his head, embarrassed. She was working on a mural downtown, full of reds, yellows, oranges. "It's my heart," she'd told me. "I'm letting it bleed on the wall."

John and I found Archie in the backyard holding court.

I moved closer to hear, John behind me. He'd hardly gotten out of bed all weekend, hadn't washed his hair, or even talked to me. Instead, he played "Lithium" by Nirvana over and over.

"Thirty years ago, a body smashed right through my roof,"

Archie told those of us gathered, "and landed flat on the bed of the old couple who lived here."

"C'mon, Arch," I said. "Right on the bed?" The whole neighborhood seemed to be there.

"Read the reports," Archie said. He kept a shrine to the accident, aerial photos of the crash site framed on his wall above the hors d'oeuvres. "I wouldn't say it if it weren't true."

John stepped forward, almost smiling, ready to run with it. "You think they had to buy a new one afterward?"

"Johhhhhnnnnn!" a few of the neighbors and I said at the same time.

He ducked when I pretended to hit him, then immediately sank back into the periphery.

Even though I knew the basics of the crash, I hadn't even begun to read everything Archie had found, so when we went back in, I was curious. Even John peeked at a few photographs. This was our home. We needed to know what had happened to our predecessors.

One article told about how melted passenger seats, a Welcome sign from over the cabin door, and body parts showered the streets. The single-engine plane Cessna had slammed into the asphalt six blocks west. All was made creepier because the current houses on our block were in the pictures, too. It was the homes behind us that were missing.

After the crash, shiny yellow police tape tied telephone poles to jacaranda trees, stop signs to fence posts, preventing the public from continuing to steal from the dead bodies—luggage, gold watches, wedding rings. Hands and feet were found on people's roofs, in trees. The neighborhood hammered signs on their front lawns for all the vultures to see: "Go away!" "Why are you here?"

John and I, arms entwined, huddled with the neighbors, gawked at the aerial photos. He lurked behind, didn't meet anyone's eyes, kept his hands in his pockets.

That the monster 727 had skidded along the street behind us, taking out houses, destroying streets, blowing the whole neighborhood up in flames, was unthinkable. Everyone at the party was distressed reading the article about the leg found in a hibiscus bush, hearing the rumors about passenger faces seen through the portholes as the jet fell, horror staring back at those on the ground, other reports calling this impossible. The group moved closer together in front of these pictures as if the increased body heat might dilute some of our anguish.

John and I tried to see beyond the grotesquery. We studied what our house used to look like—a car port, a palm tree. Gone. We ogled the old general store now turned into apartments, bungalows, 1970 Chevy Chevelles on the street. The feeling was one of awe, as if the ghosts were still with us.

I turned to a couple standing beside us because the woman kept saying, "*Dios mío!* Oh my God!" She was older and kept burrowing herself into the thick chest of the man she was with.

"You okay?" I said. "I'm from next door. Lenora."

"*Ay,*" she said, offering her hand. "Lucinda. This is *mi novio,* Ramón. He lives around the corner. I can't believe this. *Penoso!* And it happened right here."

"This is John," I told her.

"Hello," she said, nodding.

He studied the pictures a moment longer then said he was going to find Archie.

Once Lucinda stopped gaping at the carnage, she was a ray of light. Her cinnamon-colored face crinkled into a thousand crevices as her bright magenta lips turned up in a smile. She was short, though not slight, her boyfriend even shorter, though thick with ropy muscles.

"Such a nice neighborhood," she said. "I used to live nearby— Ramón's always trying to get me to move down here again." She pinched his arm.

Ramón laughed. "She lives in the middle of many gates."

"Were you in North Park during the crash?" I asked him.

"*Sí,* my brother, he out on the street." He shook his head.

"His brother died," Lucinda said, pushing hair away from his brow. "They came from Michoacán together. Very close."

"Is he okay?" I asked about Ramón as he went off to find a bathroom.

"Oh, yeah. He buries such things."

"He's lucky he can."

"We have to, *no*? Or we'd never get by."

I ran into Heather from the apartment, her strange boyfriend wearing spike earrings, a spiked leather bracelet, his mop-like dyed hair smelling of cigarettes.

"Sup?" he mumbled and kept moving through the hall. "Beer," he added.

"So what are you up to?" Heather said. She wore a short slip dress with heels so high her buttocks tilted thirty degrees higher than usual. "I didn't look at the pictures at all. Don't need it. I better go find Raymond before he gets in trouble."

"I might leave early," John said, returning with a glass of wine for me.

"You need to stay out of bed a while."

Once all the neighbors had admired Archie's succulent garden, we admired his mask collection hanging on the living room wall, many from South America and made of reeds, gourds, paper mache, and monkey hair.

"These masks explain you, Arch," said Wes, the trombone player from across the street. "You're hiding."

The living room erupted. "To hiding," a co-worker of Archie's shouted. Everyone raised glasses or cans to toast, and I did, too, thinking about how all his complaining prevented us from being better friends.

"To 70s kitchens!" shouted Wes. We'd been teasing Archie about his kitchen, remodeled in the 70s. Though neat and tidy as one would expect, he hadn't had the money to get rid of the bright orange counters, the garish wallpaper, the frilly curtains.

We neighbors discovered we were elementary school principals, telephone operators, musicians, ceramicists, EMT specialists, Planned Parenthood counselors, accountants, dog trainers, writers, and nannies. I wondered where the young married mother was, the one with occasional bruises and cuts who lived with her two sons in Heather's apartment building. Her husband came and went. She'd disappeared from the neighborhood weeks ago. I hoped to get just a glimpse of her that day so I'd know she was alive.

Archie called for the next toast. "To North Park!" he shouted, and again we all thrust our glasses to the middle.

"To praying there's never another crash," said Wes's wife, Lauren.

Of course we raised our glasses, but distress filled the room.

Lauren and Wes usually lived across the street, but left for long periods of time, renting their place out. Nobody knew where they went. Was Wes playing his trombone in another town? Was one of them in rehab? A sick relative?

She said, "If someone in your family was on the plane, how would you ever get over it? I'd want to hide for the rest of my life." Wes put his arm around her.

"But if you don't deal with it a little, how *can* you ever go on?" someone said.

Archie's masks peered over our shoulders.

Annie, a quiet woman who lived next door to Alexa, spoke up from behind. We rarely saw her husband, and he wasn't here again tonight. We felt sorry for the slight blond woman in her late twenties, figuring maybe he'd moved out, until Alexa had spotted him again.

"You can't just 'deal' with it," she whispered loudly, as if to keep herself under control. "You have to get pissed to absorb it."

John looked wan. I found him a chair.

"What good is it to get angry?" Archie said. "Especially if you can't do anything about it?"

People murmured, some seeming to agree, others not.

"Because," Annie said, louder, "you can get in a whole different kind of trouble if you don't do something about your feelings."

The background hum quieted some. We waited expectantly. What was going on at her house?

"Look," she continued, "you haven't seen Willy out much because he's very sick, okay?"

The room became even more hushed.

"If we don't admit how scared we are, we carry around a whole different burden. He could get even sicker. I could get sick, too."

The crowd broke up after that. Some went to her. Others developed in small pockets in the hallway, on the front porch, in different corners of the backyard.

Somehow Archie, John, and I found one isolated moment in the kitchen while the party blazed in the rest of the house.

"So how long you been dealing with the monster?" John asked Archie.

Archie swallowed a smile. "How long haven't I been?"

They moved on to family, and before long they were comparing beatings by Archie's brother, thrashings by John's father.

"When I got thrown against walls," John said, "they wouldn't let me go to school until the welts faded."

Archie's red ponytail curled around his collarbone as if comforting him. "Yeah, my big brother beat the crap out of me from adolescence until I finally moved out. It started when he caught me jacking off to the surfer magazines in his closet."

John and I stayed still during this conversation, partly honored, mostly horrified, until finally the trace of a smile appeared on Archie's stoic face, and we three could laugh despite the violence, despite Archie's hospitalizations, back then for his broken bones, more recently for his feelings. His own mother still wouldn't let him in the house.

John already knew about the subtle carnage of my own childhood. "Fuck them," he'd told me more than once about my parents, rubbing my back in comforting circles. The way he consumed the histories of those he cared about made me love him even more.

"My sisters sided with my mother," Archie continued, "and

thought I was gross about the surfer magazines. They ignored what my brother did to me."

John's sisters had been the ones to find his mother's body. Older, they tried to shield him, but of course how can you shield a boy who's walked in from school and found the police and his family standing around his mother lying across her bed, pill bottles scattered.

John and I wandered in and out of different parts of the party. The aerial photo of the accident presiding over the chips and guacamole was a litmus test for the soul. When I gazed into the crash site, allowing myself to live there, the thought of all those poor folks falling, extinguishing others standing in their yards, made my blood pump so hard it damaged my heart. John seemed to have so much soul he couldn't even afford to look at the photo in the first place.

Wes had been raised in the same house across the street he now lived in with Lauren. "I remember the grownups whispering over the hedges about finding somebody's schwang on the sidewalk." A beer in his hand, he said this with a look of incredulity, clearly practiced for effect.

Heather and her boyfriend howled in laughter. Annie from down the street stared. Eduardo laughed like a hyena over the schwang, though Alexa was aghast. He guffawed and made an exaggerated gesture to cover her ears, and then she laughed, too.

No, it wasn't funny. But how else does a neighborhood live alongside so many dark spirits?

By mid-October, talk of the crash had subsided. John's depression had not. A half an hour would elapse between his buttoning his shirt in the morning and then finally pulling his pants on for work. He only left the house when he had to. No matter how hard he fought, the blackness inside grew. I didn't know what to do. There were his sisters out of state, but if he wasn't telling them, should I? He stopped talking whenever I suggested a therapist.

He paced, the spark gone from his eyes, sighed so much I felt guilty if I wasn't constantly at his side. "I'm trying," he said. "I talk to God, I pray, I write affirmations every chance I get."

A month later, I came home from work and couldn't find him. The television was on, the air conditioning, all the lights. His car was parked out front.

"John?" I called into the backyard.

On my second trip to our bedroom, I opened the closet door. He was sitting upright with his arms around his knees wearing underwear and his Rolling Stones T-shirt.

"What are you doing, honey?" I asked.

He shrugged.

I reached down and pulled him up. We lay on the bed.

"When I went somewhere dark as a kid, it made me feel safe."

We turned to face each other, kicked the bedclothes out of the way. Despite the heavy stubble on his cheeks, his size, he looked fragile.

"Do you feel unsafe now?"

"I force myself to make calls at work. I want to drive away and never come back."

Our toes curled around each other's, our knees touched, our foreheads smashed together so hard there was an overwhelming sense of each other's presence. We hadn't made love in months, but at this moment, our toes seemed more important. Sometimes I was deluged with sexual feelings. I'd start to reach for him, but that wasn't really John across from me, not the one I'd had trouble keeping my hands off at the beginning.

"Should you go to the hospital?" I asked.

I already knew the answer, and you couldn't make someone go unless there was eminent danger. Any doubt and insurance companies make the decision for you.

"No," he said. Instead, he prayed to God under his breath to make himself a better person. He told me one night as we watched a show about serial killers, "At least I'm not that bad."

So I worried even more. Why would he think he was even in the ballpark of that bad?

There was Archie at the door again a few weeks later. Since he had no apparent grievances this time, I stepped outside with John behind me.

John's foot drew half circles in front of him. Abruptly, he said, "Now I'm the one feeling the gloom. I can't shake it."

Archie glanced his way. "You on antidepressants?"

"Always."

"Come over and talk sometime."

Before he left, Archie asked us to please bring our garbage cans in sooner on trash day.

By that time, the monster had swallowed my husband whole. He couldn't sleep, concentrate, get food down, remember, or forget. When we went out to dinner, he didn't speak. I dragged him to a play, but he couldn't follow the plot. He hadn't seen Abby. He kicked one of the dogs. Suddenly he'd sleep thirty-six hours straight. His boss called. I didn't know what to say.

He took solitary walks around North Park to get his endorphins going. "It's weird," he told me when he got back. "It's like I can't tell the difference between me and the outside world, like the same problems out on the street are going on inside me. A spiraling vessel shrieks to the ground, the trees are burning, fruit sizzles on the branches. Hands are hanging from telephone poles—the smell, faces missing, the earth churning like an earthquake. I can't tell whether I'm awake or in a dream."

One afternoon after he'd gone over to see Archie, he said, "He seems to have a new boyfriend." I'd seen the Volvo parked out front, a handsome older man coming by. Archie still made time for John, though. I felt left out when John came back with more energy. Hadn't I been the one trying so hard with him? They strategized about how John could get through this.

By December he was talking to God more frequently. I didn't know whether it was normal for Christian people to expect voices to talk back, but it frightened me. I was afraid of what he might do by himself in the middle of the night. What would become of me if he fell apart? Who would I lean on? I didn't want to be that alone. I couldn't do it.

When I read his journal, it said, "I am a good husband. I am a good brother. I'm smart. I have friends. I am good to my friends."

One day he returned from work at noon. I didn't have to leave for night school until later. He went straight to the couch and lay down, turned on the news.

"They sent me home," he said eventually, clicking off the set, pacing the perimeters of our little casita.

"Who did?" I looked up from the papers I was grading.

"The newspaper. The editor."

I waited, guessing I didn't want to hear this. Instead, I pondered our house built just before the Great Depression with crown molding, original wood floors, funny built-ins like the mailbox door that opened inside with a crystal knob. John opened and closed it, opened and closed it. He rubbed his hands over his face.

"What happened?"

"There's a new fact-checking system on the computer, and I don't know how to use it."

I watched him though I didn't want to see. I'd heard him talk about this new program, about what a hassle it was, about how he'd gotten along just fine without it.

"If it's part of the job," I told him, "you have to ask someone how to use it."

His hands in his pockets, he couldn't stand still. "All the techs know how to do it, so I don't see why I do."

"Look, I'm good at computers. Maybe if someone showed us, I could help." I worried more. What if I had to start doing part of his job as well as my own? Or if he got fired? How would we manage?

My mother called, and John walked away. "Everything okay, honey?" she said.

"Sure," I told her.

"Are you telling me the truth?" I heard her set her glass against the icemaker, loud chinks escaping down the tunnel for her sherry. This had been common since my father left us.

"I've got to go now, Mom. Lots of papers."

John strode to the back bedroom to lie down. He didn't get up. He ate no dinner. He wanted me to lie down, too, to not get up either. I called in sick.

"Do you think you should go to the hospital, honey?" I asked later. I didn't know how I could go to work the next day, how I could leave him here, vulnerable.

"No."

I emailed his sisters across country, told them he needed more attention, someone who could help. They emailed back that I was doing a great job myself. And then, later, first one of them called John. Then the other.

"Yes, I've been praying," he said into the phone. "I've been asking God for help."

I slipped into the bedroom where I couldn't hear, lay down, tried to think about what I'd plant in the garden come spring.

As I dressed the next morning, I asked him, "What are you going to do about work?"

"I don't know."

The cats and dogs, overjoyed we were still home, that we hadn't abandoned them to another long boring day, were unable to sneak food or sleep on our pillows.

"Why don't you take a break?" I said as we sat on the living room couch. I combed my fingers through his curls, kissed him all over his face. "Call in sick for the next few days. Relax. Get better." I didn't want something bad to happen at his office, but I hadn't thought it through enough. What would he do with all that free time?

He phoned the newspaper.

"Are you sure you don't want to go to a hospital?" I asked. Prepping for my afternoon class, I'd reread the same line about Ambrose Bierce's character hiding from the enemy, but every time I got to the end of the sentence, I couldn't remember the beginning.

"I think I better go," he said, not gazing up from his Bible.

I put my books down and called the insurance company before he changed his mind. They referred me to mental health. Mental health referred me to the insurance company. I tried the hospital, but they wanted me to call the insurance company. Finally I called John's doctor who got him a bed, but it wouldn't be ready until 8 p.m.

I took John to work with me. I couldn't leave him at home. What might he do? He stayed in the library while I faced my class, called students by their wrong names, finally confessed I had a relative going to the hospital and couldn't think straight.

Concern broke out on their sunny, young faces, like it would for anyone in a dire situation. They didn't know John like I did, though. They couldn't possibly understand, maybe no one could, how much I loved him. Because of his wiring, I never had to explain feeling down or afraid, crying, temporarily hating myself, being different. He understood. He loved me anyway. The chemistry we'd had when we met had been usurped by the monster. I fantasized about having passionate sex with other teachers, the dog groomer. I won arguments with myself about how you couldn't blame someone in my situation for having an extramarital affair.

After teaching, I found him in the stacks. "Maybe this is all really stupid," John said. "Maybe I'm not that bad. Other people don't have to go to the hospital."

"You need to go, John."

We waited an hour in the intake office. When the nice nurse came to interview him, he began to cry. I rubbed his shoulder while she and I made meaningful eye contact. We knew he needed to be there, but we didn't want to scare him away. An hour later, she took him up to his room. I wasn't allowed to go.

When she got back, she asked me about my background, my family.

"I guess I'm afraid of being alone," I told her.

"You're alone now, honey. From what you've told me, you've always been alone."

For some reason this shocked me. It played inside like a rim shot, the unstable metal hiss shrieking on and on, reverberating throughout me. I thought about the years with my father, the years without, taking care of my mother, now John.

"Don't you believe he'll get better?" I said, more loudly than I intended. Why was she working here if she wasn't going to be more helpful?

She smiled, seemed to assess me. "I doubt he's ever been completely stable."

"Is this hospital going to do him any good?" I stood, my eyes watering. Part of me knew she was right, but this approach seemed hurtful. "If you're going to be so down on him, I should take him somewhere else!"

"Lenora . . ."

I held my arms, walked to the corner and pretended to examine her books. I wasn't going to give her the pleasure of caving in to her.

"I'm sorry for being so direct," she said, "but this has reached a crisis situation, he's in the hospital, and there isn't time to take things slow."

I pulled myself up straighter, then sat, but refused to look at her.

"You have to find your own peace," she said. "Somewhere inside where you can live."

I stared at my nails while she added, "You haven't picked an easy man. All I'm saying is to take care of yourself."

I nodded and left.

At home, I was so cold. Where were those sturdy arms that were supposed to keep me warm? I wrapped myself tightly in blankets, then slept through the night for the first time in months, strangely relieved to be by myself. Then guilty for being relieved. I wondered how we would pay for everything if John wasn't working. Our mortgage was high enough, but then there was the co-pay from the hospital, the doctors. Maybe I'd have to work until dementia set in and I wasn't allowed in front of a classroom anymore. I'd be moved to a home, then forget where I lived and end up on the streets with other old women who didn't belong anywhere.

I saw him in the evenings from 7:00 – 9:00, the only visiting hours. On my very first visit, he said, "They want me to have electroconvulsive treatment."

"Shock therapy?" I could feel my mouth hanging open.

"I don't want it. What if it fucks me up? What'll it do to my brain?"

I didn't say anything.

"Can they make me have it? What if they force me?"

"They can't do that anymore."

Secretly I wondered whether maybe he should have it since nothing else was helping. No one knows exactly how ECT works. Maybe it makes inner demons go haywire so they can't get a foothold. Short-term memory is shot. Probably a good thing. Some people on his floor had been helped by it tremendously.

I called his ex. John didn't want Abby to see him this like this and absolutely didn't want her at the hospital. Leslie and I agreed Abby should know John was ill, but not how badly.

Then one of his sisters called, for me instead of John. When I told her about the hospital, she said, "All you can do is let go and let God."

"Yes," I said, cringing uncertainly.

"You're already doing everything you can."

"Yes."

Tending my aloe vera and cosmos in the front yard a week later, I temporarily fooled myself into believing there were no problems and instead meditated on pleasant things, lying on the beach in Baja, seeing so much open space, blue in one direction, sand in the other, John and I strolling, holding shells you could no longer find on the beaches in California.

"Hey," Archie called. "Haven't seen John around." He hosed his yard wearing only swimming trunks in the dense heat of the Santa Ana winds.

"Around?" I tried to snap out of it, realizing I was going to have to have a real conversation. "Oh, well, he isn't doing so well."

"Is he home?" he asked, turning, like he might walk right up to the front door.

"No!"

He stared, and I couldn't think of anything to say. "He had to be hospitalized."

"Where?" Archie watered the same spot on the lawn for five minutes while we talked, something he'd have complained about if I'd done it. "What happened?" he asked.

Though I tried to explain, everything came out in a jumble, their ordering new meds, my going there at night. Many of John's friends didn't have time, though they tried to phone him. I didn't have to explain patient pay phones to Archie. "You don't know who's going to answer. If the person is on a lot of meds or delusional, sometimes they hang up."

Archie visited him the very next evening, stayed nearly the whole two hours. I wondered what they spoke of, worried again about Archie being more helpful than I was. But then I thought about what the nurse had said about my already being alone, what his sister had said, in so many words, about my already doing everything I could. I was grateful, actually, that someone else was taking care of John.

I had a late class and could only stop by at the end of visiting hours to hug him. After hiking down over-waxed hallways, riding the rickety old elevator, traveling more hallways, passing nurse's stations, people wearing hospital footies, banks of phones, and lights that were too bright, I found him in his room. "What did you talk about with Archie?" I asked.

"Nothing much."

"Come on."

Neither of us spoke, and then we slid our arms around each other.

"He said when he was in the hospital they sent him home too soon."

Two nights later when I stopped to visit, my father was stepping out of the elevator I was about to step into to go up to John's floor.

"Dad? What are you doing here?" I asked. I didn't get in.

"Visiting." He looked awkward, but then he always looked awkward.

"How did you know John was here?" We paced slowly toward the revolving front door.

He stopped in the entry. "He called from your school library the other day. He thought I should know you were going to admit him in case you needed anything."

"Oh." A good idea, though the notion of him helping me seemed bizarre. On the other hand, I supposed stopping to see my husband in a psychiatric hospital was kind.

"Thank you," I said.

We kissed each other's cheek. He left.

When I got to John's room, it still seemed absurd. "You told my father you were here?"

John read on the bed. "I thought it'd be better coming from me, so he wouldn't hate me."

"He doesn't hate you."

"I know."

I sank onto the bed beside him, leaned over on top of him, hugged him as hard as I could.

He stayed three weeks—groups, heart-to-hearts with mental health workers, psychologists, psychiatrists, nurses, anyone, trying to purge himself. If his father were still alive, I'd have shot him. One kind of meds and then another, meds that knocked him out and meds that raised his anxiety level. He refused to take the ECT treatments, no matter how hard they tried. He was too afraid. But he did get a little better. At least, as Archie had warned, hospitals always determine you're better when your insurance runs out.

One afternoon I was gardening, meditating, absenting myself from the world when I heard the friendly sound of squawks above me. The caw of the wild, the sliver of magnificence in my day, a species with enough wit to thumb their beaks at our intensity, my intensity. A trowel in one hand, a flat of thyme by my knees, I gazed up and savored the presence of the macaws, smiled as a twosome in a queen palm preened and groomed each other,

Suddenly the feet of my neighbor, Alexa, were beside me on the sidewalk. "Too bad they're going extinct, isn't it?" she said. Why did I have to be polite in my own yard? I didn't want to see anybody. But I also wondered why I felt this way around Alexa. I might not have admitted it to the woman at the hospital, but I really didn't want to be alone. I needed friends.

"Extinct?" I said, rising, though I knew it was true. Our North Park macaws, jesters, freedom seekers, AWOL from countless enclosures, truly were social beings, not just here for show. And now their homes were disappearing.

"Don't they love each other for life?" she asked. I saw now that she'd painted her own t-shirt, bright blue on black.

I nodded. "They make life-long commitments."

I stepped closer to Alexa, and we marveled over the birds together.

When John came home from the hospital, few in the neighborhood knew where he'd been—Alexa and Archie. His truck had roosted on the street all that time. Each household must have had its own theory. Engine problems? Europe? A gambling junket?

"You have to get better," I told him, collapsing next to him on the bed. "I love you."

"Why?" he mumbled into my neck. "I'm nothing right now."

"That isn't true."

"The whole thing is unfair to you," he said, placing his chin on my head.

Days, he went to an outpatient therapy group. The hospital dispatched a bus for him, returned him home afterward. The patients called it the Happy Bus. Nobody wanted him driving on the new meds. He was discombobulated. I drove him everywhere.

"He's an asshole," John said after group one afternoon. "This leader is just trying to make me angry. He says I'm holding everything in and getting depressed instead. He picks on me."

I wondered, but decided to stay out of it.

"He wants me to get enraged, but not too enraged. Reasonably enraged."

"Maybe it's a good idea."

We stared at each other until we both laughed a little.

"*Bitch!*" he shouted.

"*Bastard!*" I shouted, chasing him to the kitchen where we panted over the countertop.

A few weeks later, he started his car for the first time, took himself out for a haircut, got an oil change, the fluids filled.

Leslie and he arranged for Abby to be dropped off at our place one afternoon. "Daddy!" she said, running up our front steps. She jumped into his arms.

"Hello, kitten," he said, carrying her inside.

"Did you miss me, Daddy?"

"I really did."

Archie stopped by a few nights later. I stayed out of the room, listened. They got on the subject of John's family, how his mother, until she killed herself, defended him from his father.

"She was an angel," John told Archie as I considered a paper discussing rhyming "cutlets" in the other room.

"Clearly not," Archie said. A tough love approach? "Not if she left you behind with him."

"Shut up!" John shouted. "She always cared about me. She loved me."

A smirk in his voice, Archie said, "You have to work on this hero/villain thing. He fed you. She ran away."

"She didn't run away. She died. And it was his job to feed me. It's the law!"

"I know, John. I know," Archie murmured.

"Everything okay out there?" I called from the bedroom. Pushing my papers aside, I got up and joined them.

"Everything's fine," John said.

After a minute, he explained, "Dad thought he was doing right. Did I tell you he owned his own appliance store? Down there fixing things until all hours so we could have a good life."

Archie glanced his way. "Who can recover from anything with so many unhappy ghosts on the property? The house itself is angry. All those dead bodies." He looked at both of us. "Sometimes I burn sage and walk my property."

"What does that do?" I asked.

"Relieves the spirits, lets them know they're sacred, they're part of the land, but they can't keep haunting me."

Lying in bed that night, John confided, "I want to wake up okay and then stay okay instead of the same boulder lowering onto me every morning."

After our three-week separation, it felt good just to have him there to hold. "I swear you're going to be okay, John," I said. "You have to be."

Before too long, I knew we'd make love again. Whether everything worked the way it should with all the medication was irrelevant. At least we were together in our little house.

There he was again a few days later, Archie at our screen door. By now I thought nothing of pushing the dogs out of the way as I threw the door open, crisp winter air crawling through our casita. John continued fingering B.B. King's "Ask Me No Questions" in the living room.

"Hey," I said to Archie.

But today he made no movement toward the porch, let alone coming inside.

"You know," he said, "I really don't appreciate it when you park on my lawn."

"You mean *my* lawn? I don't."

"Yeah, you do. I know it's your lawn, but we agreed I'd take care of it because it's in the front of my house."

"I don't park on the lawn."

"You do."

"I do not. I park next to it." I gravitated back inside, tried to get behind the door when suddenly John appeared and moved in front of me.

"Okay, it's your lawn," Archie said, his face screwed up and ugly, "but sometimes when you park on the driveway, you're only feet from the front of my place. Since I'm the one watering, I don't like it getting brown."

John stepped further forward, now on a mission, cocky. "What's the problem?" he said, his voice too loud.

"She's parking on my lawn."

"It isn't your lawn, and I just heard her tell you she didn't park on it. Stop bothering her."

"Step back, John," I said. "He's not what you're angry about."

Archie's voice became too loud. "You're overreacting. You're crazy."

"Get the hell off our property. Now, man!"

"John," I said. "This isn't what you want to do. Remember what that doctor said. Only Archie's not who you need to blow up at."

Archie smiled, the slight sneer working across his pale freckles making me sick. He held out a plastic grocery bag full of oranges from his tree, the nicest neighbor in the world.

"Thank you," I said, though I didn't mean it.

"It's just that if you park on it, I can't keep it green."

With that, John stepped all the way outside and stalked right up to the thin, red-haired man, nose to nose. Despite John having forty pounds on him, Archie didn't flinch. He probably didn't believe John would do anything. I wasn't so sure. Something was clamoring inside John, something was coming to a boil.

"Did you hear what I just told you?" John said.

"Hey, man, she shouldn't park on my lawn."

John pushed, and Archie's arms shot upward, dangled. Oranges cannon balled, rolled down to the street. I saw John step forward again, and he hit Archie this time.

"Stop it, John!" I shouted.

I threw the metal screen open so hard the knob cracked the stucco on the side of our house. I ran straight for him, jumped, put my weight into it. We fell hard on the driveway, hitting a grease spot. "You can't do this," I yelled.

John smiled, dumbfounded.

After all these months of me being the sane one, it felt good to let go, so I didn't get off him right away. I couldn't take care of all of this myself. Archie was more than welcome to try.

He now stood behind my car where he had a good head start to run home if need be. He peered around the back fender. There was blood on his lip, slipping down his neck.

"Good work!" he shouted at John. "Now you're talking."

He kept the car between us a few moments longer, no dummy when it came to this sort of assault, until finally he walked around and grabbed my hand to pull me up. Then John's.

John must still have been feeling the deep sting of rage because then he told Archie, "Don't complain so much, man. We're tired of it. If you don't stop, I can't say what I'll do."

"It was a small request."

John's plumage began to fall until he was just a guy standing on his driveway. "I don't know why I pushed you, man."

"Hey, I'm telling you—it's the ghosts," Archie said, so infinitely sure himself.

"You think?"

"Absolutely. They're still with you. You have to make peace with them."

"Yeah, I know." John brushed off his jeans and nodded his head.

"Imagine our fences on fire," Archie orated loudly, "the blast shrieking into your house, coming to get you—fragments of humans waiting to be loaded onto those refrigerated vans. Some folks weren't ready, couldn't let go. You have to appease the spirits, man, so they'll leave you be, or you'll get stuck here with them."

John appeared bewildered. I wanted to take care of him, but he was the only one who could get the plane off the ground again.

Suddenly coming to life, he said, "Do you think we could walk our property, too, like you do on yours?"

"Sure."

They set off to Archie's for the sage, like he'd never punched Archie or made him bleed. They returned shortly, the piney, medicinal scent of sage following them.

I stepped back from the whole thing, went inside, a pure, sweet exhaustion enveloping me. I leaned on the tile of the kitchen counter so I could watch their progress from the window.

John pressed his nose on the screen right in front of me with a wicked smile. "You make sure they don't all come running inside."

"No ghosts allowed," I said.

He made a show of giving me the bushel of sage. "For the radiant maiden whom the angels named Lenore."

"Only this, and nothing more."

We kissed through the screen.

The two tall men paced the backyard, first the burly one tracking the boundaries of his land, the slim red-headed one pacing behind, the dogs barking, the cats following, even two green macaws looking on from a satellite dish. The men would make it to the other side now. They chanted something melodic, their hands clenched around smoking sage, and I saw my husband close his eyes, now given over to the anointing of our North Park property and praying for everything and everyone who'd ever tried to live here.

Uncle Rempt

He arrived from South Bend on a Thursday. Small and hunched over, Uncle Rempt had a bald spot on his crown shaped like the yin and yang symbol—a backward S in a circle, a dot of hair on either side.

"Car trouble," he said when he showed up at our place in Aloha, Washington. "I was on my way to a nifty little place a chum's been telling me about in California—North Park—but I decided to swing by Aloha and see my baby brother first." Here he smiled at my dad. "Had to play tuba at a roadside joint to buy the new radiator. How are you doing, missy?" he said, turning toward me. Though shy, I couldn't help laughing, at least until my father glanced my way."You must be Susan."

"Ever tell you about my old pal Neil?" Uncle Rempt asked Dad. "Navy pal, until he shipped to Pendleton, then stayed on in Cali, married his sweetheart Sabrina and had two sons. The four of them live in this sweet piece of heaven, warm and balmy all year round." Looking at me, he added, "I hear the two boys skateboard everywhere they go."

"You gonna sell crystals?" my kid brother Brad, fourteen, said with his best you-some-kind-of-idiot? sneer. I was nineteen, and we all knew about the colorful rock crystals Uncle Rempt was so crazy about. Even if my dad didn't talk to him, we'd heard rumors from our grandparents.

"Yep," Rempt went on, as if there were no awkwardness, "thought I'd get myself a little shop going here in town for a while, see some family, save a little cash. Then I'll be moving on to North Park."

Uncle Rempt winked, his elf body now doing a 180 so we could all see "Area 51" written in metallic silver on his t-shirt, a small spaceship flying near the neckline, under his blue velvet jacket. Facing Brad, he said, "You must have yourself a fine business raking in all kinds of loot." My uncle swished the hair on Brad's head back and forth in a way I knew my brother hated.

It was all I could do not to laugh again, what with Brad's blotched red coloring indicating he was riled. Then Rempt caught my eye, smiled, reached behind my hugely curly hair, and brought out a baby chick.

"Oh!" I said, delighted.

"Get that thing out of here!" my dad said.

Rempt's opposite, Dad was tall and paunchy at forty-six, though he too had a bald spot, which I now realized looked like jail bars, black rows of hair across white skin.

"You can't stay here," Dad said almost immediately, and gave his brother directions to the Super 8 Motel.

After my uncle had left, Dad told us at the dinner table, "Haven't seen Rempt since '02, the year they caught him practicing medicine without a license."

"How does he know how to heal people?" I asked.

"He doesn't."

We were eating fish and chips, like every Friday. I was on my best behavior because now that I was a junior, Dad was considering letting me live in the college dorms senior year.

"Geez, Dad," my brother said, "the school's Catholic and she's a frigging accounting major and the dorm's all girls. It's not like she's going to get knocked up. She hardly even talks to her boyfriend."

Mom, diminutive, blushed. "Everybody got a napkin?" she asked.

While she and I tried to be invisible, Brad, who Dad thought was a scream, heaped up a forkful of slimy fries, oil glistening from the tines, and said, "I'm going to college early if I have to keep eating this junk."

Two days later, Dad slammed through the front door after visiting the little shop Uncle Rempt had rented. "The scoundrel's sleeping in the store room with a bunch of colored glass, for god's sake."

"All that glass must be pretty," I said.

"You stay away from there."

On one of our twice-weekly dates, my boyfriend, Michael, also Catholic and studying accounting, looked up toward Jesus at the mere mention of crystals. "You didn't tell me about *that* part of your family," he said. After graduation, Michael planned to marry me, and then we'd move to Whitefish to work at the credit union and have two children.

"Uncle Rempt?" I said. "He's one of my favorites." We were sitting in a Denny's, a place Brad said was safe since it was public and we wouldn't be tempted to do anything untoward.

"Susan, I don't think we want someone like that around our kids."

"How many did you say we're having?" I said, sprinkling my fourth and fifth packets of sugar onto my waffles.

"Susan!"

"Two, that's right. Two." I laughed, withdrawing my hands quickly from the sugar bowl.

The crystal store opened a week later. I got right over there without telling anyone. The place smelled of sandalwood.

"Susan," Uncle Rempt said, hugging me warmly.

"Wow." I gazed spellbound at a jasper green stone splattered with red.

"Bloodstone." He folded it into my hand. "You need to keep the thing, sweetheart, living with that brother of mine. Could be the most important crystal out there, and you went straight for it. The stone of courage, they say. Destroys the walls of prisons, opens all doors."

Quartz, tiger eye, and amethyst sparkled under glass cases. Prisms made of aquamarine, topaz, and tourmaline hung in the window, the sun penetrating the translucent stones, warm color bathing my face and arms, peacefulness.

"Crystals are essential," he told me. "Humans have lost touch with Earth's magic."

I was too overwhelmed with gratitude to respond.

Dad grumbled about Rempt's gems every chance he got. "Reminds me of the time he ran away," he said later that week. "The police found him in Miami conning women, saying he'd make them porn stars. Never figured out where he got money for the plane ticket and camera. That's when the folks threw him out the first time."

"Good lord," Uncle Rempt said the next day at the shop. "I was seventeen, and my girlfriend paid for everything. She wanted to be in *Playboy*, for heaven's sake. The girl made me lovesick, but I couldn't get her to stop posing."

Leaning quietly against a wall made of only drywall and a little putty, thumbtacks and crystals hanging here and there, I asked, "You mean . . ."

"She wouldn't stop spreading them," Rempt said, sitting down in the only chair, his head in his hands, unnerved. "Under the table at McDonald's, in crowded movie theaters, when the gas attendant came over to check the oil. The police caught us visiting Santa at Macy's."

I let my back slide down the drywall, sank low with my uncle. "You mean . . ."

"Spread them right in front of all those little kids and their mamas and grandmas. The rent-a-cops took us both in. She was only fifteen, but I was underage, too, so they just called our folks. My parents wouldn't even hear me out. Never let me explain. They immediately thought the worst. Your father wasn't much help. They sent me to the YMCA, but the place wouldn't let me check in because I wasn't eighteen. I slept on the streets for weeks."

Seeing he was about to weep, I stood and patted his shoulder, went to make him tea.

"Yeah, I can't be around your father for too long. Soon I'll join up with my Marine pal I was telling you about in San Diego, the one who's all settled in that little piece of paradise. He's out there running an oxygen bar on the side of his crystal business. I need to learn it. Oxygen's remarkable, revives body and soul. His prices carry some real fine energy, too."

I looked out into space and tried to imagine the ocean. "Dad thinks there's no reason to leave Aloha."

"Susan, sweetheart. This isn't a real life."

"I know."

So then he heated up the rest of the tea for me.

I smuggled myself over to Uncle Rempt's place every chance I got, assisted him in understanding his clients, released myself from everyday life to see where the crystals would take me. I asked women what really made them happy, what they really wanted to do, and who or what was keeping them from doing it. I started answering these questions for myself and moving even further into Uncle Rempt's camp.

Over the next few months, he sold water sapphires and amber and onyx to opulent ladies with French manicures and diamond tennis bracelets, guiding one to higher awareness, another to a place of serenity, a third to let go of the heartbreak of losing her baby. I saw what Dad was talking about, yet what I noticed most was the women leaving happier, calmer.

That fall Dad rewarded me for my high GPA with a pre-owned Toyota. The family waved goodbye as I drove off to live senior year in the dorms. When my parents went back inside, Brad turned and flashed me a moon.

But once I'd moved in, Dad called relentlessly. "Are you getting enough sleep?" he asked. "Are you eating right?" One night he called and said, "Have you started buying thongs?"

"*Dad!*"

"Your mother wanted to know."

"It's none of your business."

"Everything you do is our business."

"I wish I wasn't sleeping or eating enough," I told him.

"What are you talking about, Susan? Do I need to drive over there?"

"No."

I didn't explain that I only wished I fit into the dorms better and, like the other girls, drank instead of eating, gorged on brownies after a few hits of chronic. If only I were invited to a party, I wouldn't have to admit to sleeping so well. But I doubted I'd be happier. The other girls dished under their breath about my tennis shoes since I refused to wear heels, about how all my clothes were red and green now that I wished so fervently that the colors of that jasper stone would free me. They stared tirelessly at my wildly curly hair, hair I did continuously less to curb.

Then there was the day in history class when my professor finally questioned my obsession with the Darwin Theory.

"This is a Catholic college," I told her, "so you have to teach creationism. But what do you really think?"

"This isn't . . . ."

"Anybody can see that chimpanzees' hands are the same as ours. Dolphins talk like we do. Who's more empathetic than a dog?"

"Susan . . ." And then she let us all go early.

Recently, I'd brought the subject up with Michael, who said, "Oh, Susan." And I never could tell whether he meant, Oh, Susan, obviously these animals are just like us, or, Oh, Susan, of course we don't believe in this kind of thing.

One day when I turned the corner to Uncle Rempt's crystal shop, I saw that Dad had snuck and parked the family car down the street. They were all waiting inside when I got there.

"Why are you here?" Dad asked the minute the crystals over the threshold started chinking. He was sitting on the folding chair, glaring at the worn-out door, waiting for me. Mom pretended to be invisible, standing in the screened area where Uncle Rempt slept. Brad pocketed a few gems while we talked.

"What do you mean what am I doing here? He's my uncle." I didn't sit down. I certainly wasn't going to stay for this.

"We're filling out applications to become spiritual coaches, Bruce," Rempt said. "Great school in North Park, San Diego. We're also looking into oxygen."

"Right," I said, and the two of us cracked ourselves up laughing. Dad didn't.

"You think that's funny, Rempt," he said, "because you never had kids."

"You think all she can hope for is to be a teller in Whitefish and live with a man who doesn't see the heart in this girl, who doesn't see what a beauty she is inside and out?"

"For the love of God, Rempt," Dad said. "I don't want her over here. Clear?"

"She's getting older," my uncle said. "How long before you stop telling her where she can be?"

I felt for my dad, who clearly didn't want to acknowledge that I'd never be the princess he'd hoped for.

That night when I got back to the dorm, Dad had left a message on my machine: "We've cancelled the payment on your dorm. We expect you home for Friday fish."

I called Michael. "Let's move in together now and see how we get along."

"Has that dorm made a she-devil out of you, Susan?" he asked.

I packed up everything the following day, even the teddy and thong I'd bought just in case Michael was more fun than I thought he was going to be. I took a last look around and decided I wouldn't miss the place at all.

I left a voicemail saying I'd be staying with a friend in town collecting for a mission to Honduras so they wouldn't start looking until my trail cooled. Uncle Rempt thought the Corolla made us seem more legitimate, and we ate jelly beans just as colorful as the crystals all the way to North Park. Uncle Rempt tucked his haul of gems all over the car—the trunk, the glove box, sitting in the rear window over the trunk. Truck drivers boomed their horns at us, small children flashed us peace signs out the back of minivans. We were never going to stop.

People Scream

A piercing sound travels down the long, waxed corridor at the Center for Life, where behind every door an Anonymous meeting is in session. Heather holds herself still at her receptionist desk when she hears it. Even though it's not the first time, she stops breathing, like maybe she can see or feel where the unsettling cry is coming from. For this one minute, listening, she is alone. Afterward, she'll tally tonight's donations on the computer even faster than usual so she can get out of here, but still she feels panicky.

She's mostly alone in her apartment, too, though Lenora next door is pretty cool. It's not like they're best friends. Lenora must be ten years older. She lives in a real house, right below Heather's apartment. Sometimes she lets Heather lay out in her backyard to soak rays.

Who would make such a noise at the Center? Is the person okay? She's not sure where it's coming from. Alcoholics Anonymous? Gamblers, Overeaters, Sexaholics, Narcotics, or Rageaholics Anonymous? Did his wife leave him because he couldn't stay out of Vegas? Is he fat, in debt, horny, a wino?

She can't quite get comfortable in her mini and her new red espadrilles that tie around her ankles, so she keeps crossing her legs and recrossing them. Members walk by, eyeing her nose ring and the tats on her arms, but she tries not to care. After all, these people are old, in their thirties, some even in their forties. And they have problems, something Heather hopes she herself will never have. For now she just can't wait to go clubbing with Raymond after work.

"Did you hear that sound?" she asks a woman hurrying past. She asks because sometimes she feels like there's a moat between her and the rest of the world, and she wants to make sure somebody else heard the scream too.

But the woman just smiles a fakey smile, shrugs, keeps moving.

Tonight has been like most Wednesday nights at the Center for Life. She passed out envelopes for donations. The regulars filed through, and she gave them guarded smiles. She wishes she were home in her apartment. From her vantage upstairs, she has a view over the whole neighborhood and feels like she knows those people, especially after going to the party for the anniversary of the plane crash.

At the Center, the one she thinks of as Rug Man winked and jerked his head as he went by, making her wonder why the rug didn't come flying off. Why he didn't just shave his head like everyone else these days she doesn't know. Then came the one always carrying a briefcase and wearing white, who she thinks of as the Efficiency Expert. He walked by her desk three times, dragging his finger over the fake wood, thinking she didn't notice, then, as usual, stopped to ask the question: "Can I get a receipt?"

"After the meeting," she always tells him.

"You look stunning this evening."

He's so lame. He says that every Wednesday night.

Even Wally from Poway, north of San Diego, showed up, wearing his United Parcel uniform, rolling his eyes and saying he'd come to put in his two hours.

But by the time she hears the shriek on this Wednesday, it's 7:30 p.m., and everyone is inside the rooms, and the hallway is all but deserted.

Heather took the receptionist job at the Center because she thought she'd meet more interesting people—well, men—than she did at City College. More mature, more worldly. But sometimes she thinks that on Wednesday nights the place should be called the Center for the Dead, what with the way people walk around licking their wounds, glassy-eyed, on the brink of falling apart. Besides, now she's met Raymond, and she's about to change her major to art. She'll fit in better in art. And Raymond likes the sound of it.

She steps outside to smoke a cigarette so she won't have to listen to the scream anymore. She supposes she probably does look pretty good tonight because she's just had her hair shaved from the level of her ears on down and dyed the tips of the rest of it mauve in anticipation of switching to the art department. And she's wearing a new pleather jacket, violet, that looks like leather but isn't from dead animals. Raymond thinks it's cool.

As soon as she steps back inside, she hears the shriek again, and the old memories come up. It feels like a scream she's always wanted to scream but has never been able to allow herself to. The sound is clear, but tonight it's bottomless, a moan from the depths of the belly, and it goes on for longer than seems possible, eventually fading out into a dry whimper. It sounds like a dog throwing his head back and yowling at the moon, a train flying through the mountains and riding the horn, a baby desperate to be held.

She doesn't want to think about either the sound or what's causing it.

She swims to the other side of her moat, sorts her receipts by room number, stamps personal checks with the Center's stamp. Most of the groups send in a check or two, except for the debtors' group. Their envelope contains only cash.

Heather's tats and her hair, which she messed around with before leaving the Center, don't seem quite so unusual later at Myth, a rave club in an abandoned warehouse in the Gaslamp Quarter of San Diego. In order to find where Myth moves every week, you have to be cool enough to have the phone number. Even that changes occasionally.

She's glad Raymond came and picked her up from work because something foul-smelling is going on inside her own vehicle that she can't figure out—a rotten piece of fruit under one of the seats? A moldy sandwich?

"So how was work today?" she shouts over Narcoleptic Youth's song "I Can Be a Bitch If I Want to Be a Bitch," mainly because she wants him to ask her. Raymond especially likes the band because they skateboard on stage.

They're leaning against a waist-high, two-person table. Raymond helps train dogs, takes them to local convalescent homes where he lets them shake hands and be petted, have their ears and chests scratched, which for some reason cheers people up. He takes a class once in a while and says he wants to have his own business, though Heather doubts it will ever happen.

She thinks of one of the many times during the sixteen years she lived at home when her father said he was going to open his own garage. Humming an old Beatles song one morning, he toasted himself an English muffin, a slice of margarine waiting at the end of his knife. He checked the liquor cabinet to see whether he'd have to go out that day while Heather read the back of a cereal box.

"Yup, hon," he said, "a few more years of this nine-to-five shit, and I'm on my own."

Heather nodded, only briefly glancing up from the box.

"Nobody breathing down my back anymore, nobody okaying my vacations . . ."

When he wasn't talking, he hummed "I Am the Walrus."

"No more dirty fingernails for the old man . . . know what I mean?"

He knocked the cereal box away so she couldn't help seeing the oil stains on his hands.

Raymond waves his hand to get the cocktail waitress's attention, the blue streaks in his hair catching in the brilliant bands of light. At first Heather thought his impatience meant he was a born leader. Lately she's had trouble resurrecting this fantasy.

Heather shouts, "The screamer screamed again tonight. It's so loud. I can't figure out who's doing it."

"Some poor bastard." Raymond makes a clicking noise with his mouth. "Hey, you want me to go have a talk with somebody or something?"

"*Raymond*—somebody's just unhappy."

She sighs and goes back to watching people dance. She's learned in the short time she's known him that he's from a family of men who drink too many beers. When they play horseshoes, they burp and then say things like, "S'cuse me—must've been someone I ate."

It's 1:30 a.m., and Raymond and Heather have arrived at Denny's earlier than the others. Two young girls, maybe seventeen or eighteen, have scooched onto the orange vinyl in the next booth over. Both have blond hair. Both are slender. They glance over at the mauve on Heather's tips and quickly look away. They're with a man who's about forty.

Heather wishes she could hear their conversation better. The blond girls seem so normal. Maybe she'd get the answers to some of her own family questions. Maybe she'll bleach her hair blond. The three are fairly animated: first laughing, then shaking their heads, then making vehement assertions they all seem to agree on. The latter is what makes Heather doubt the man's their father. Why would they tell him about something that really matters? She hears a lot of loud whispering, something involving a friend they haven't seen. One girl starts crying.

Heather stops herself. *Of course* the man could be their father. Girls like this—soft brown eyes, barrettes in their neatly parted hair, cardigan sweaters—have fathers they can confide in.

Soon enough two other couples Raymond knows join them.

"Where'd you end up?" one of the guys says.

"Myth," says Raymond. "Woman wasn't having a good time, so we dogged it."

Rose the waitress has stalked by several times scowling, on the verge of telling them, as she always does, that they can't have a booth unless each of them orders. Rose, so old she has to be eighty-seven, must have started in her tan Denny's uniform before any of them were born. Heather can attest to the last six years, anyway, since that's when she turned sixteen and got her license and started driving over for coffee to get out of the house. She can hardly stand to look at Rose, whose life seems so squelched that she cares more about the number of Splenda packets people use than anything else. Heather imagines her going home to a studio apartment above a bar, where a neon light flashes blue into her living room and the closet contains nothing but Denny's uniforms.

"*Raymond*, Rose is on her way over again," Heather whispers, wondering why she has never before seen how juvenile he is.

"Relax, babe. You're giving me the creeps," Raymond tells her.

Heather scoots out of the booth. In the parking lot she sniffs back tears. He always wants to tell her what to do.

Then she notices Wally from Poway pushing his way through Denny's revolving glass door, alone. He isn't wearing his United Parcel uniform she saw him in earlier, and she thinks he looks okay. Of course he isn't her type. Though who *is* her type escapes her at the moment. She pretends to be looking something up in the Yellow Pages of a phone booth, watches Wally take a seat at the counter.

When she was nine years old, she used to sit at the Denny's counter with her dad and order waffles. Just the two of them. He didn't turn poisonous until later. By the time she was seventeen, she hardly heard anything he said. She went underwater. The words he sent her way turned into sound waves, diluted by the time they reached her. She moored her deepest thoughts and dreams, rarely letting them drift to the surface, only vaguely into the real word. When anybody spoke to her, unless she really concentrated, she only caught about half what they said. People were always asking where she was, what continent, what planet, what universe.

The moat worked for a long time, but lately it seems to be drying up. She can't get away from the world; the part of her that matters seems unguarded. There's all that screaming.

"Heather!" Raymond says, on his way toward the phone booth. "C'mon."

Under "exterminators" in the yellow pages, Heather sees Lloyd's Pest Control, Pied Piper Termite and Pest, The Terminator. "I'm not going," she tells him.

Raymond sidles up beside her. "Whaddaya mean? How you gonna get home?"

"I'll manage," Heather says, her eyebrows arched. That's why she should have driven her own car, so she could leave when she wanted, but then she remembers her car has that smell of rotten oranges, day-old garbage that has turned up out of nowhere and won't go away.

Suddenly getting rid of Raymond becomes all-important. "*Leave*," she whispers.

"Fine," Raymond says, his face bright red. "Like I need this."

And before she knows it, he and his friends peel out, trailing smoke in the Denny's parking lot. Even though she told him to go, she never really expected to be standing here alone.

She looks up "Taxicabs." Yellow, Red Medallion, Bill's.

Through the glass of Denny's, Wally is engrossed in his newspaper, enjoying a burger and fries. She guesses he must not be in Overeaters Anonymous. Unless this is a binge.

"Hey, Wally," she says, standing beside him now.

Wally jumps, folds his newspaper, wipes his mouth with a napkin though it isn't even dirty. She guesses he's uncomfortable around women, that it's not a Sexaholics meeting he attends at the Center.

"What are you doing out so late on a Wednesday night?" she asks.

"Second job. Started doing a little bartending to pay some bills. How about you?"

Heather stares at his mustache. He doesn't sound like he's in AA or in serious trouble with debts. Would she be able to get him to shave the mustache if they became involved? Would he try to tell her what to do? If they got married, would he keep the second job?

"Look," she says. "Could you give me a ride home? It's not far—North Park, just off 805, south of University. I had a fight with my, this guy . . ."

Wally seems nervous. She wonders if he's married. Maybe he's got kids at home asleep.

"Isn't that where the plane crashed all those years ago, the one that ran into the Cessna?"

Heather nods, and he says he'll give her the ride.

They're in the alley behind Denny's, and Wally's unlocking his beat-up Dodge hatchback. There aren't any Legos in the back, but now she sees he must be older than she thought. Thirty-five? There are his ZZ Top cassettes to consider, and his mustache is so 80s. Thirty-seven?

"Do you have kids?" she asks.

"Two," he says, before climbing in and slamming his door twice before it will shut. "Wish they lived with me, but they're with their mom. See them all I can. "

Before she gets in, she hears a scream from down the alley. Maybe it's a cat. Maybe it's a woman. She's never thought about the sex of the screamer before. In fact this scream in the alley doesn't sound so different from her own voice.

She hears it again. Frozen, fascinated, she looks over at Wally, who is watching her listen. It's a thick scream, a knobby scream, from the depths of someone's—or something's—being. It's the scream of two girls out with a boy who's driving his Pontiac too fast, a cat who has been treed, a woman giving birth to a child. It's the scream of someone who's won at the lottery, a man finding his dog dead of old age on the back porch, a woman jumping from the car after her husband slapped her for being too friendly with the waiter.

The air afterward is tight, too quiet. Heather's ears are attuned to the slightest sound.

"Getting in?" Wally asks.

Then she remembers where she is and she does get in the car.

"Did you hear that?" she says.

"Someone screaming," Wally says, shrugging.

"It just unnerves me."

"So where you headed?"

She gives directions. She says, "Have you heard the person at the Center? Every Wednesday night someone screams. It's a loud, horrible scream. None of the doors open, and no one ever comes out."

"People scream," Wally says.

They drive for a while. He hasn't lit a joint yet, so she doesn't think he's part of NA. What will he think of her majoring in art? Most likely that it isn't practical. She wonders how he'd feel about a career in nursing.

"Tell the truth," she says. "Don't you think those people at the Center are mental?"

They're at an intersection, and Wally glances over at her. Like four hairy caterpillars, his eyebrows and mustaches all rise in unison when he smiles. He's not so bad looking: He has a hot smile and only the beginnings of a beer gut. "You're young," he says. "People get weird as they get older. It's too much work to keep trying to be normal, and you can't help being weird after all you've been through. It's better to accept it and move on."

Heather studies the awnings, shops, and gas stations as they get closer to North Park, then, as the hatchback accelerates, stops concentrating at all and allows them to blur into a long fuzzy streak. "Don't you think it's strange," she says, "that none of those people have anything better to do than go talk to complete strangers on a Wednesday night?" Vaguely, it dawns on her that maybe she shouldn't be saying this since Wally himself goes to these meetings.

"Is this where I turn?" he asks.

Heather nods, points: "It's that apartment building. The guy next door? I think he was in the hospital. He said the apartment used to be a grocer's in the 30s."

Wally tips his head to one side.

"And can you believe that little strip of bright green lawn? Right there. My landlord just painted it. Can you believe he'd paint the lawn?"

"A lot of people are looking at why they're unhappy," Wally says. "A lot of people aren't satisfied and they want to know why. They don't want to sit around and pretend like their parents did. Right here? In front of this old station wagon?"

"Yeah," Heather says, and then she laughs. "That's my old clunker."

"People take what they can out of those meetings and leave the rest. You're the one you have to live with. You're the one who has to be able to stand the thoughts in your head."

Wally parallel parks, then turns and says, "Do you know you left your window down?"

"It's been broken for months. I want to sell the car and get a better one."

He pulls on the hand brake, cuts the ignition. She wonders if this means he'll walk her to her door, try to kiss her.

They face each other in the old bucket seats, the gear shift their only obstacle. "Nice, quiet neighborhood," Wally finally says, one of his elbows leaning against the steering wheel, the other over the back of his seat.

She sits tall. She doesn't want to slouch, like her father used to complain of. She sits tall so she won't look dumpy, shakes the hair around her face.

They lean forward, closer. She's sure they're going to kiss—the moment, the quiet. She imagines a time not too long in the future when he'll love her so much, think she's so beautiful, he'll follow her into her apartment. They'll undress with only the street light shining through her windows. He'll help pull out the sofa bed, unless they're too passionate to wait that long.

"I think someone's in your car," Wally says, stepping onto the street.

"What?" Heather's in another world, in her apartment with her clothes off, stroking Wally's head while he suckles her breasts, his brows and mustaches brushing against her chest.

But Wally is already inspecting.

"Someone's in my car?" she says. She hesitates, checks to make sure her clothes are really on, then jumps out after him.

She's not sure whether the explosion she hears a couple of blocks over is a gun being shot or just the backfiring of a car. Why do loud noises, screams, seem always to follow her?

Wally leans down, peers inside the station wagon window. When he suddenly throws the door open, the dome light illuminates an older man curled on her back seat. He has a dingy blanket over him, and there are plastic grocery bags everywhere, stuffed with newspaper, aluminum cans, clothes, and food.

"Oh my God!" Heather says. "My God, who is he? Is he dead?" She pulls the sleeves of her pleather jacket down over her hands, the collar up over her nose and ears. If only she could disappear. What must Wally think? She has to make it clear to him that this isn't normally how her life is, that sleazy things like this are out of the ordinary.

But Wally is laughing. "Looks to me like he's had a few," he says.

Heather shrieks at the man, *"Get out of my car! This is my car!"*

Wally lifts her by the middle, carefully places her several feet away on the sidewalk. "Take it easy," he says. "Unless you know who the guy is. You don't need more problems."

"I'm sure! Of course I don't know who he is. I don't know people like this."

Wally heads back to the car just as the old man sits up in the backseat, scratches the dark film over his face and neck, the only parts of his skin they can see. "What's happening?" he says.

"Time to move along, champ," Wally tells him.

"Sure, okay." The man flings old newspapers out the door, three tattered coats, a piece of cardboard. His smelly blanket follows. "No harm, no foul," he mumbles, tying his shoes. "Just a few nights."

"No way!" Heather says. "He's lying," she tells Wally, but even as she's saying it, she knows it's true. The funny odor in the car now makes sense, as does the bag full of aluminum cans she found on the back seat last week that she couldn't remember putting there.

"Get out of my car!" Heather shrieks again, breaking out of

Wally's hold. She socks the man in the shoulder and the chest. She doesn't know how people get like him, but she has to fight back to make sure it won't happen to her.

Wally pulls her away again, and she's crying. "Did you smell my car?" she yells. "He's the one who should be in AA. He's the one who needs help."

The man straightens up from tying his shoes. "There ain't no help for this, sweetheart," he mumbles. "This is hell we're in right now. There ain't no help for human beings. Could you hold her a minute, bub, while I go get my cart?"

The man scurries off down the alley—long gray hair, not putting much weight on one of his legs—and returns quickly with a Walgreens shopping cart. Taking more bags from the car, he stacks them on the sidewalk, just like she does when she's been shopping, then disappears quickly around the corner.

Heather feels a gentle hand on her shoulder. "I'll walk you to your place," Wally says.

She sees the blueness of the television flickering at her landlord's. He leans out, his hands on his screen door just below his porch light so that she can see his cuticles are stained green.

"Everything okay?" he calls. He probably watched the whole thing from his window, will probably think of something she did wrong or try to charge her for having a roommate since the guy was sleeping in her car.

Wally waves the landlord away, and Heather wonders why a man who has to be nagged about fixing leaky pipes cares so much about how green his lawn is. It's like her own father, wanting to be sure the pails were wheeled in the second the garbage men emptied them, meticulous about his hibiscus, always the one in the neighborhood to put out a flag on holidays. If you could make things look right, maybe no one would notice the rest. She's beginning to think it's crucial that she mention what's going on underneath, the things that don't get said. She's begun to think she's going to have to speak up or lose it, tell people how they can treat her and how they can't if she wants to feel better, stop worrying about the moat. You can't permit strange men to live in your car; you can't pretend it's not happening. Even thinking this makes her stand up straighter, feel more in control.

Wally is laughing on her front porch. "Were you listening? Did you hear what he said?"

"Who?"

"The landlord. He saw the guy take all the bags out the other morning and then put them all back that night, but he wasn't sure whether or not the guy might be some relation to you."

"I'm *sure*," Heather says, too angry to look at him.

Wally continues laughing, but he lets go of Heather's arm.

"How do people get like that old guy?" Heather wants to know.

"It'll be okay," says Wally. "Just move the car in the morning."

He follows her up the stairs to her place.

"I just want to look out your back window," he says. "I think that's where the plane crash happened."

She leaves the lights off so they can see better, and they peer through the east window. She wonders if he'll try something up here.

"See right there, where all the new buildings are?" he says.

When she looks, she notices for the first time that the homes do seem different.

"Those are the ones that went up in the late seventies," Wally says, pointing. "Look at the sliding glass doors. That one has a hot tub."

She wonders what that day was like.

"Cool area," he says. "All the old houses from the twenties and thirties."

"Sometimes macaws land on that telephone wire right there. I even recognize some of them, like there's an olive-colored one with red on his head."

Wally nods.

She gazes at the homes below. "Sometimes I hear people arguing. Seems like an arguey neighborhood."

"Everyone has problems."

"There's a couple that lives right down below," she says, pointing next door. "Sometimes the husband, I think he used to work for the newspaper, lies out in the backyard at night when he thinks nobody's looking and stares at the stars. He's kind of strange. I like his wife, though, Lenora—the one with the geraniums. Then there's these skateboard brothers who get pretty loud across the street."

Wally doesn't try to kiss her good night when he leaves, doesn't even ask for her number. "See you next Wednesday," is all he says when he leaves. Heather wonders if he thinks her life is full of busted car windows, fights at Denny's, that she actually likes her job as a receptionist.

She locks and chains the front door, pushes a chair in front of it, closes all the windows in her apartment tightly. She isn't going to let anybody hurt her ever again.

The next day she skips classes, then calls in sick at the Center. All they have is swimming lessons that night anyway, and a fencing class. They'll get along fine without her. She spends the day watching television and staring out the window to make sure the old man doesn't come back. She can't afford to have men living in her space without asking.

That night she parks the car two streets over, then calls in sick Friday as well. She spends the afternoon at City College, careful to make her appointment with a different counselor than the one who helped her change her major to art. She wants Wally to see her as smart, practical.

She lies low over the weekend, discards so many items from her closet that she feels she's starting her life over. She sprays her car with deodorizer more than once, changes her nail color from black to red, neglects to answer the phone. Or at least she would if it ever rang.

Finally Wednesday rolls around. She takes great pains with her appearance. Gone are the mini and high-heeled espadrilles. Gone is the vampish cerise lipstick. Instead she wears tight blue jeans (Wally will love them), leather boots (her feet can breathe!), a bandanna tied around her head like a pirate's (only the mauve tips show).

Her Wednesday night people have begun to show up. Heather watches them carefully as she gives directions and answers the phone. She wants to know why she's been able to live through so much—moving out on her own at seventeen, taking care of herself from then on—and yet these people can't seem to get through their little problems. She wants to know if there's a pattern as to who goes in which door. She thinks it can't be just random.

There's Rug Man winking as usual. She smiles and so he lingers a bit. She's thinking he's not so bad; she could make him feel more comfortable about his balding, get him to shave. She could consider a career in psychology.

Just as she loses sight of him, there's the Efficiency Expert making his second trip by her desk. He drags his finger down the fake oak, has begun to ask a question when the phone rings. He tells her she looks stunning, but he'd probably prefer her in a clean, tailored suit.

When she looks up again, there's Wally from Poway.

"Cheers," he says, brightly. Could he be going to AA, after all? He leans against her desk, asks how she is, checks out the fit of her jeans.

Sexaholics Anonymous?

"You know, I'm embarrassed," Heather says, "about the other night. The man sleeping in my car. I have no idea how he got there."

Wally smiles. He really is hot. "Forget it. He's no more desperate than the rest of us."

"I didn't want you to think . . ."

"Oh, I don't think anything," Wally says. "Feel like getting something to eat later? I got the night off from tending bar."

She's going to say yes, of course, but then there's a loud noise at the entrance, so she turns and sees that someone's umbrella is jammed in the revolving door. He pulls and pulls but seems stuck behind the glass forever. She knows Wally's still there as her phones light up. She answers three calls in a row, gives directions, information, advice.

Then she looks up. Everyone's gone. Behind all of those doors. Even Wally. Which door did he go through? All she can see is row after shiny row of black and white tile. She can hear the clock make distinctly separate ticking and tocking noises when the halls are this quiet, this still. The hallway reminds her of the long tunnel of her adolescence, of being completely alone, of knowing no way out, of having no one to care.

She's prepared to stay open somewhat; she's never going to shut down as much as her father did. But she's got to bridge the moat.

She glances around, afraid of what she knows will happen, what she knows she will hear. She can still call Myth. The club is always there, no matter what has gone wrong. She dials the number. She still has a few outfits she hasn't thrown away. There's the plastic dress, a roll of stick-on tattoos. She could still go home and roll a skirt up short. A man answers, but before giving her Myth's current location, he wants to know who she is.

Suddenly she can't think of a thing to say.

The line goes dead, cold. Could he really have hung up on her? After a whole year?

Then she hears it, the scream, the inconsolable cry of a child who has lost both her parents forever, a girl irretrievably alone, a woman trying to accept this but who still yearns for something more. She has to command her legs to hold her a few more minutes as she runs down the slippery, waxed hallway.

Which door did Wally go in? Which door was it?

Then she sees that it's not important, and she picks a door, any door.

Sea Life

The motel room door is wide open, the beach only yards away. Just inside Sean tries to chill on a yellow plaid chair where wet bathing suits have dried and whisky has spilled, where people have had sit-down sex, legs entangled in the wooden arm rests. He wants to focus on the booming of the ocean, but his hangover magnifies a dread already lurking. Early Monday morning, tomorrow, is his first in a line of interviews for a job he doesn't want.

He wishes he could be as laid back as his brother, Matt, primo North Park skateboarding partner, or as his buddy Kyle, who lies on an unmade bed across the room in front of the TV. Above Kyle, a chipped oil of King Neptune gazes fearlessly into the unknown, his trident in one hand, his conch in the other, announcing young sailors crossing the equator for the first time, or whatever line they may be crossing.

Sean's head throbs not only from last night's ecstasy, but from the nameless infinity he faces now that he's spent four years getting A's in classes he didn't like for a degree he wasn't sure was his idea and has ended up with a girlfriend who wants to buy matching dinnerware. The girl in the apartment down the street back in North Park, Heather, seems to do whatever she likes, and she's not that much older than he is. She ditched the one guy with chain earrings who smoked weed on her balcony and is all over some new guy who runs around in brown shorts and a brown truck. Why can't he have a life like hers?

His mother will be torqued if he doesn't march out there and get a job already. When she dragged him to the thirty-year anniversary party of that plane that crashed all over the place, he said, "I wish another one would freaking fall out of the sky so I could move on and do what I want."

"Don't you *ever* say things like that."

"Ah, Sabrina, he's just a kid," his dad said.

More recently an old Navy chum of Dad's, Rempt—a funny-looking guy, short—had moved into the hood after Dad told him what a little piece of heaven the place was. Sure, it's heaven if you want to be bored into oblivion.

Now the guy lives in a mother-in-law apartment with his niece in the next block. Did this guy Rempt ever have some kind of plan? The niece, Susan, is hot letting all her wild curls grow out into what are practically dreadlocks. What does her uncle care? The guy wears metallic t-shirts and crystals hanging from his neck and tries to sell people oxygen.

In the motel room at the beach, Kyle's honey, Tina, says, "Let's go, sweetie," as she glides out of the bathroom, blushing in a string bikini and heading straight out the door. Kyle shoots from the bed, his grin going frisky.

"Wowza!" he calls over his shoulder as he follows his girl into the parking lot.

Sean can't help laughing at his buddy. "Yowza!" he calls back.

"Wait up," Kyle tells him.

"We will."

Tina smiles as they cross the parking lot to the back of Kyle's father's 4 x 4 where they'll do the deed.

On Friday before they left for the weekend, Sean told Kyle, "We have to take your dad's truck, man. The license frames." The frames say "Pacific Beach," proof the truck is from the coast, making it tougher for local surfers to peg them as outsiders. This way the couples won't return from the waves to find "wankers" spray-painted on their vehicle, their tires slashed, the windshield shattered. Though they all live inland, each has a mandatory surfboard, angled against the motel room wall in various colors and shapes, like a line-up of crayons.

"Sean?" Iylette calls from the bathroom. Suddenly she's furiously sweeping the joint.

"Who cleans on vacation?" he asks her. The ecstasy has almost worn off, though his brain still hurts, and he's got that insatiable thirst that comes afterward.

Pouty, Iylette brushes up around his feet.

No matter how much metal Iylette has pierced through her skin—her brows, her nose, her belly—he likes the soft hairs at the back of her slender neck and until recently the comfort she offered. All weekend she's plied him with homemade banana nut bread, massages, and coy smiles. It's not comfort he's yearning for, though, but signs of life. Something might die inside if he can't see beyond the habit of life, if he can't see some kind of shimmer out there.

Locals consider their group "Surf Kooks" who don't know their asses from the Pacific Ocean. It's far worse being from North Park, fifteen miles east of the beach, than from Kansas City. Both hail from land-locked states of mind, but the pasty inlanders are expected to have at least a clue about surf etiquette. Yesterday Iylette lost her board, bonking a surfer on the head. "Why don'tcha go make me a batch of cookies?" he shouted, following her. Today the couples have decided it's safer to at least start out at the beach together.

"You don't have to do this," Sean says, as Iylette sweeps into table legs, spilling glasses.

"Somebody's got to take care of things."

"I told you, it's my fault, not yours. I don't know what I want, and until I figure it out, I don't think it's a good idea if we're quite so . . . serious."

"Whatever."

Her body stiffens and her cute little lips stick out. He watches her rifle through his clothes, straightening, always straightening.

At first Iylette's pierced tongue and the two-inch plugs lodged into the lobes of her ears made her seem like a soul mate, a person who yearned for an edgy peninsula of a life, still vaguely attached to the mainland, but dexterous enough to transcend it. Now he knows everything about her pierced little boy nipples that so intrigued him at first, how to fondle the stud in her clit enough to grow huge and eager. But they don't want the same things.

"Relax," he says, patting the mattress beside him. It's not that he doesn't like her. Last night he saw her talking to some guy from another motel room, and it definitely upset him, but he has no right to say anything in his current state. She glares at him from under the pierced gold hoops of her eyebrows, then throws herself down next to him so close his body slumps with her weight. Her feet perch on his lap. Part of him would like to rub them like always, but he's afraid of encouraging her. He hopes Kyle gets back soon.

Waves boom and plunder so close there are droplets in the air, a sliver of bliss—the ocean. No parents. No pressure. Freedom.

Or at least the elements of bliss are here. Doom laps at his little corner of paradise with tomorrow morning's interview. Once he gets a job, what matters to him will be irrelevant. He'll be expected to work the next sixty years of his life, the next 21,900 days, the next 31,536,000 minutes, driving bleak freeways, wearing stiff clothes.

They turn to the TV, which has been watching them all morning, focus on the news woman who wears a high-fashion blue suit and a complicated blond hairdo even though what she's discussing is the surf. Smiling, she stares desperately off camera, trying to see the teleprompter. This seems to happen to all adults— they only say what others have written for them. The woman's eyes are startled, surrounded by tentacle-like lashes of stiffened mascara. Something poofy and frightening has happened to her lips that has caused them to swell and look like female genitalia.

Sean can't quite close his mouth, mesmerized. "You think she's ever seen a wave?"

He puts his arm around Iylette's hips, a good fit after all this time. They shake their heads together as if they are watching a new mammal at the zoo. For the moment they are *simpático*.

But then there's a rap on the door, and they see a fresh-faced girl their age with a sun-streaked ponytail standing in the threshold with a maid's cart. "You ready for some cleaning?" she asks, her freckles starfish-shaped against one of the sunny panes of her face. "I'm Cathy."

Sean thinks she's cute, especially when she steps inside to see the day's surf report.

"Wow!" she says, ogling the TV ocean, her brusque smile broadening at the sight. "They're breaking shoulder-high. They were only two feet at 5:00 a.m."

Iylette stiffens on his lap. Sean doesn't want to care how she feels.

"5:00 a.m.?" he asks. He notices too late he's dropped his arm from Iylette's waist, something he will pay for. Immediately she stalks across the room, and snatches up more bathing suits and bottles around the place.

"I surf every morning before work," Cathy says. "They let me make up the time in the evening." She smiles right back at him, her healthy brown arms crossed over her chest.

He allows himself to imagine it: surf, work, water. Whenever he likes.

Cathy's mop falls over, and he stands to pick it up for her. He can't help noticing how her skin glows, how strong and hard her body is, the salt smell of her silky hair.

"We don't need you!" Iylette bellows, her broom handle perilously close to the girl.

"Iylette," he says. He grabs her.

"It's cool," Cathy says. "One less room."

As Iylette throws the broom at his feet, frantically wipes down counters, the maid cart rumbles and squeaks away.

And then, thank god, Kyle and Tina bustle back into the room. Kyle hoots, "Surf's epic out there, man! Let's go!"

Sean jolts, happy to hear sounds of life from his buddy while Iylette snaps shut the hollow bathroom door, barricading herself inside.

The Pacific Ocean heaves and hisses outside. Sean, Kyle, and Tina gather their equipment and take off running. Sean glimpses gulls flying to the shoreline as well. When he reaches the beach, his toes grab fine white sand and kick out wisps behind him. Sandpipers skitter in small packs. Kids body womp on boogie boards.

Then he's off into the real stuff, the soup, the depths, *whoosh*. He throws his board on the glass, his body on top, one shoulder over the other, paddling and thrusting into deeper waters.

The three stay together at first, try to blend in so they won't get vibed by locals. Heedful of wave rights, they avoid collision with other surfers by propelling themselves around instead of through desirable breaching waves.

No matter how hard they're trying, though, it's difficult not to notice that the serious surfers—the real surfers—all wear solid black board shorts, not striped or purple. The crayon-colored boards also give Sean and his buddies away. No wonder the slimy guy at the surf store gave him such a discount on the turquoise board. Every surfboard ridden by a local is white.

He wrestles through white water, flings himself over the falls, moves out to one edge. Salt water gulps up his nose and his head starts to clear. The sun feels good on his back.

He monitors the others off in the distance. Kyle rides a wave in. Then Tina. Cautiously, Sean catches a wave, too, but he hasn't fully enough assessed the boneyard, the area where the waves break, and he winds up right in the path of an advanced surfer who's forced to cut out of the wave he thinks he's conquered.

"Chicken or beef?" the surfer shouts, far too close to Sean for comfort.

Sean has been yelled at enough to know he's being given an

ultimatum: He can either fight over the waves, "beef," or skulk out of the way, "chicken." Sean quickly skulks. He doesn't need a local board shot into his gut.

He pushes farther out to sea, not caring where he's going as long as it's away, floating, pitching this way and that in the big black pool. When he's reached a comfortable point of isolation, he retches and his hangover immediately dissipates.

He rises and falls, drifts to an even less populated area. The locals surf by the sand bars where the waves are better. It's not just the waves Sean has come for, though, but something purer, something in nature. He allows himself to slip aimlessly away into whatever it is.

Whole communities of beings go about their business underneath him—schools of mackerel head north. Even with the seaweed, he can see gills, tails, eyeballs peeking out of kelp paddies, hiding from the terns and pelicans that swoop down and gulp them. A diaphanous jelly fish floats like a see-through parachute. Millions of anchovies, sardines, grunion—bait food— shimmering everywhere.

He allows his vision to blur on a droplet or a fish, prisms of sunlight turning pink and green and blue. Everything is a little too quiet.

A dude on a long board floats by, skin a radiant gold that comes from living in the water and on the beach, not like skin from North Park. The surfer's hair is flaxen and bushy from salt water. Heavy white cream coats his nose and lips, but you can still see thick red skin peeling underneath, freckles forever imprinted. He nods pleasantly, which makes Sean feel lucky.

Until he sees the fin knifing right at him.

His eyes automatically focus, and Sean screams.

His feet leap to the top of his board from where they've been straddling over the sides. He's let himself go so far inside himself that it's hard to come back. He knows about sharks showing up now and then in warm waters.

He screams again. It's involuntary, nothing he'd ever want

anyone else to hear, not locals or inlanders. But who hasn't seen the bits in the news about those ravaging jaws, the love of the kill, the ability to smell even a single drop of blood, the five rows of teeth ready to mangle, shred, and rip somebody's leg off? Who hasn't seen the news shorts about people who *have* lost legs? The girl surfer who lost her whole arm a few years earlier? Whole human bodies being dragged out into the deep for a private meal, never to be seen again?

Punch it in the nose. That's what you're supposed to do. Punch the shark in the nose to disorient it. Sure . . . and then the fin shoots right past him, turns back.

His buddies, inland, see it, too. Tina screams. A few other kooks abandon bright-colored boards, make a small exodus from the water. Jaws. The majority who stay put, their calves still dangling at the sides of their surfboards, can't have seen the *Discovery* shows Sean has, the monsters with the agitating jaws, throwing themselves aboard boats, swimming so close to shore they can grab swimmers' ankles. His heart pounds and he shrieks again in sheer horror.

Even Kyle. Even Kyle screams, holding his board in front of him as he runs backwards to shore. And that's when Sean starts to notice the locals laughing. Guffawing. Whistling. Gloating.

Not until later will he remember that only his group and the other kooks did the shrieking. Those who stay in the water, those in black trunks on white boards, position themselves for more rides in the surf now that the waters have been temporarily cleared.

Despite the terror, somehow Sean's board has turned around so that he's pointed out to sea. His neck and ankles are as alabaster as the other kooks' now standing on dry land, but he is too far from shore to effectively flee. He tries amid it all to keep his feet up.

Suddenly there are fins everywhere. A nightmare. Godzilla meets King Kong. Fleetingly, Sean thinks that there are worse things than living inland. What's a little boredom?

"Hey, you weenie!" It's the surfer dude, the one on the long board who floated by so nonchalantly earlier. He's shouting at Sean, laughing at the same time. "They're not sharks!"

The dude throws back his head like it's the funniest joke he's heard in a long time, and Sean feels just like that, a weenie.

"Whaddaya from the sticks or something?" The guy starts coughing to catch his breath. "We don't want to have to rescue you."

Sean jerks his head, cool as he can. His headache may have evaporated, but he's going to puke again. His arms hum with electricity to paddle back in. He'll make it to shore. He'll get away. He won't die. He doesn't want to die.

"Dolphins!" the dude finally spits out. "Bottlenose. You kooks," he tosses over his shoulder as he floats away.

The fins charge closer and closer. *Dolphins* doesn't sink in right away, and besides—sharks, dolphins, who cares? They're too fast, they're prehistoric, they weigh over 500 pounds. They're almost on top of him, and he's heard dolphins can bite, too. He's out of here. But he's so clumsy, so hurried, his foot slips back into the water.

He's never had so much respect for the world before. For plain everyday life. For the earth. For the ocean. Shore seems so far away. His life will be different after this. He promises himself. He'll go out and get a job immediately, forget about his hunger for understanding life. He won't take what he has for granted. He'll appreciate.

For a brief, cogent moment, Sean sees Kyle and Tina on shore. They're standing still, unmoving, like they can't take their eyes off him. Kyle's standing behind his board. Tina is behind him. He even sees Iylette with that motel guy. They're all standing in a mass of seaweed. Flies must be biting at their skin, but they don't move. At least he's still on top of his board.

Two gray fins are coming right at him. He's never seen anything alive move this fast. They can only mean to menace, or what would the hurry be?

But then they split. One fin goes around him one way, one the other. They miss him by millimeters. That's when Sean sees one of their goofy faces looking back at him. He lets go a little. Goofy. Gray and white. Beaked. Big eyes on either side like an enormous but friendly collie. The grin. Like he's laughing at Sean. He or she. But she's too big not to take seriously. She could crush him.

He sits up on his board, pulling his knees as close to his body as possible. He's seen dolphins on screen, he's seen people swim with them in parks, he's read about their occasional interaction with surfers. He's heard about how they communicate with echolocation, about how in rare cases they've bounced it off humans who have lived to report a sense of elation afterward. She's too big to experiment with, though.

He's never seen anything like this. The two animals shoot past him out toward the sea again, join up with their pod. And then he sees a row of them, and it's like a water ballet. Nothing is more beautiful as they body surf together, on the same curl, nose first, in perfect symmetry. Then each kicks out of the wave, leaping out the back, in unison.

Finally he lets go of his legs. They sink into the water on either side of his board again. He's too tired to hold them up. There are at least five of these enormous creatures when he counts, most far off and surfing, like a row of humans. Their beaks protrude from the inside of tubular waves, their dorsals direct them.

But there is the one that hovers, rubbery and sleek, swimming around him. She won't go away. She clicks like an overgrown cicada and barrels her body, rolling over and over horizontally. There seems to be a shadow mimicking her every motion, and it's not until this smaller apparition barrels, too, that Sean sees she has a calf. Spray shoots from her blow hole when she surfaces. A shorter smaller spray issues from the calf. The little one is four feet long compared to her eight. Their blow holes open and close. Breathing. The mother is so powerful when she shoots by it's spellbinding.

She glides away, then back again—and the calf does, too, in concert. Like any mother in the wild, whenever her calf drifts too close to Sean, she shepherds him away. But then she turns back and clacks and rattles and clicks, makes creaking sounds, whistles. Every time her head surfaces and he can see, she's got that dopey smile on. Guileless. Ridiculous. Sincere.

He feels honored, a diplomat to the sea. He knows this isn't common, that dolphins don't careen up to human beings to visit unless they feel utterly safe. The dolphin must know he's a good person, that he only wants peace. Simplicity. Freedom. He reaches his palms into the liquid velvet, launches himself and his board further away from what he knows, toward the horizon, realizing this dolphin is less menacing than many of the humans he knows. He's moving up the coast with the currents. If only he had fins. If only he could survive in all this water on his own.

She flits out ahead of him in a way he'll never be able to propel himself, to depths it's humanly impossible for him to go. She rides high up on her back, like she's walking on water, grins and makes noises like she's laughing. So does her calf. She's entertaining, having so much fun herself. She's laughing at him.

The ocean is no threat to them, a liquid oasis for their pleasure. Not a deep dark hole where one could drown. They loll on their backs, white bellies up, until finally he laughs with them. Here he is, lying on his board, drifting in the Pacific, and smiling at a couple of Cetaceans with goofy curved grins. Why would he ever want to go back to land?

Sean cries but he's not sure why or where the tears are coming from. The mother remains curious, exploring Sean, so close he could touch her. It's almost like she's trying to say something. He drifts for a long time, dead weight, into the sea.

He wakes up, further out than he remembers. Shadows on shore have started to elongate. He doesn't know how long he's been out there when eventually he notices gray, amorphous figures on the beach he knows to be his friends from North Park casting their arms back and forth in the air, trying to get his attention. Somewhere on another plane, he remembers Kyle's father saying they had to have the truck back by 3:00. Getting home is so massively irrelevant that it hardly registers. He can still make it to the job interview first thing in the morning. He pushes his torso up off the board and waves them away—*leave me here, go away, goodbye*. Kyle knows him. Kyle will understand Sean wants to stay. Iylette won't. He can hitch a ride back later. His buddies float away like a mist, out of his mind, out of his vision. They no longer exist.

He feels so good it's frightening. He doesn't think he could ever have wished for more than he's feeling now. Even if he doesn't quite know where he is or how he's going to get back to shore. The current has pushed him to rockier waters, where there are reefs that cut, waves that pull. Even though the mother and son have floated off, he sees the mother's eye directed at him, only on one side, piercing, knowing.

Then he feels it again, only this time it's stronger and he's sure. It's a texture, a pulsation, a signal. It's a locomotion, a singing inside. He's never felt such euphoria. Sound travels up and down his legs; his insides pulsate, echo. Lying on his stomach on his board, he never wants to pull his arms out of the sea again. It's ultrasound, the magic fingers on a vibrating bed, a jet flying over and causing the Earth to tremble. The dolphin pushes from the water, that goofy smile. Only it's not goofy. Not at all.

The little dolphin jumps up and slaps himself down in the water. His creaking giddiness is all Sean needs to let go, to leave his board behind, swim toward the mammals, not quite sure where he's headed, not quite caring if he can get back.

He's a good swimmer, Sean, and he wafts along with the breeze, floating, side stroking, in a trance. He loses sight of his board, though he knows he was wearing a leash. The sun moves further west; the tide rises. Mother and calf play games, race to and from their pod. They circle Sean, shoot out of the water, splash. They circle him, giggle, creak. It's an anthem, a chant, a hymn, a lullaby, so natural he doesn't hear it anymore. He floats up and down over billows and surges, close to sleep. He's worn out, the treading, the exhilaration. He needs to get back.

His muscles hurt. He's hungry. The wind has made the water so choppy he swallows a mouthful of salt water. Where is he?

It's starting to get dark. The sunset has caused red veins to bleed through the smoky clouds. He's cold. He's shivering. His legs are cramping.

He coughs, tries to keep his head above water, then turns to float on his back again. How will he get to shore? Don't fight the current, he tells himself. Swim across it. But he has to get to land. He swallows another mouthful of sea water, coughs again. He makes one of his hands push, then the other, transporting himself closer to land, his motel room.

He sees the dolphins one last time, the undulation of their water when they turn and head back to sea. They plunge into the depths, soar skyward through booming waves, noses airborne, curve, and head straight down again, loping their way back to sea. Abandoned, Sean manages to watch their silhouettes as he himself dog paddles to shore, their dorsals, until they're only another set of gray triangles mixed in with the rest of the pod and finally could be mistaken for the gray waves themselves.

Spent, he beaches. He knows he's drifted up the coast, but he lies there until he's so cold he has to get up.

The others have left, as he wanted them to. The room has been cleaned, empty beer cans gone, a layer of sand vacuumed from the carpet, the trash emptied. Only his clothes lie on one of the beds.

There's a beauty about the emptiness. He's not going home. He doesn't have to. He's got enough money for at least a week. So he'll miss an interview.

He glances down the walkway, sees Cathy, the girl who surfs first thing every morning. She's finishing up her shift, watering aloes by the office. Maybe he'll ask her out for a beer.

What is there to stop him?

This Time of Night

We're sitting on plastic picnic chairs in our backyard as the sun sets. Willy is grilling swordfish for dinner, and we're planning a camping trip to San Onofre State Park. We're going on our maiden voyage in the 23-foot trailer we just bought.

"Is the campsite right next to those two big concrete things?" I ask Willy. The evening is as close as it can be to darkness while still being light. A lingering red strip of sun hangs over the trees and roofs in North Park, and our dog tries to align himself with us humans as much as possible, thinking he might get a bite of something.

"The boobs?" Willy says.

Everyone in Southern California calls the big concrete mounds on the San Onofre Nuclear Plant near Camp Pendleton the boobs. It is as if a giant woman is lying face up on the beach, exposing herself to the elements. I shake my head. "Wouldn't be so funny if something went wrong up there. Wouldn't be so funny if there was an accident."

"Okay, okay," Willy says, "'the containments,' then. What's with you, anyway, Annie?"

I know this isn't really what's wrong, and it makes me even madder that he knows, too.

The girl in the apartment at the end of the block, Heather, waves over at us from her balcony in clear sight from our backyard.

I wave back. Her UPS guy seems to have practically moved in, no secret since his big, brown UPS truck is always on the street. He seems okay, though always tired. Heather says he's got three jobs now. Fortunately, she can't hear us talking quietly on our patio. Not too many know all that's going on with Willy and I, at least they didn't until for some reason I blurted out that he was sick at the anniversary party. Thankfully, no one has said a word about it since then. It's hard when a friend figures out what specifically Willy's illness is, that he has AIDS, because then I have to take care of her while she recovers from the news. Things may have changed since the eighties when the disease first came on the scene, but there's still a stigma attached even if people want to pretend there isn't. Now in our late thirties, we want to be treated normally as long as possible before Willy's disease gets worse.

We also say hello to Alexa, the woman who paints, and her husband who is from Mexico, since they are out in their yard next door, too. Sometimes she brings murals she's working on out back where they can dry better. They're pretty wild, splashes of all different colors. Alexa and Eduardo don't seem to spend a lot of time together.

"So what do the boobs contain, anyway?" I ask Willy.

"If there's a nuclear accident," he explains, nudging the potatoes with a poker, turning the swordfish, "they're supposed to keep radioactivity from escaping into the atmosphere."

"So what are those concrete nipples at the top?"

He shrugs.

"Great place to go camping," I say, "right under some radioactive boobs."

"When it happens, it won't matter how far away we are. No one will escape."

I tell him, sighing, "They just caught that serial killer up there, too, what's his name. We're going camping in a place where serial killers get caught."

His disease is more controllable now than it was in the early days, but because Willy was diagnosed late and seems resistant to many antivirals, his prognosis isn't good. He must have contracted it in high school when experimenting with IV drugs.

Willy gazes up at the moon as he shakes his head so slowly I finally smile. I love it when he makes dinner for the two of us.

"You've got to stop focusing on things like serial killers, honey," he says, standing and taking the fish off the fire.

"What else is there to focus on?"

He retreats quickly into the house with the food without even looking at me.

A trailer is for when you need to get out of your own life for a while and experience something else. Just buying one is a huge act of faith on our part since Willy's health has already begun to deteriorate.

When he heard the price of the trailer, Willy knew something was wrong. "People don't sell 2006 trailers that cheap," he said. We'd been hoping to find an '00 or an '01.

And it seemed funny that there were still vacancies at the San Onofre campground when we called a week ago. Funny because it's right on the beach, a haven for summertime campers.

"Maybe," I suggested, "it's because of that serial killer. People don't want to be so exposed. They want to be able to lock the windows against a person like that, bolt the doors."

"Who's going to be afraid if the guy's already been caught?"

"I am. About all the other ones still out there doing it."

We drove down to a friend of Willy's dad's to look at the trailer. We took Willy's dad, whom we call the Chief, along with us.

At Stu's mobile home, he and his wife Cissy were sitting in a room they'd cordoned off to trap the air conditioning. The lights were off and a John Wayne movie played on a large flat screen TV. Even though they were standing to answer the door, you could see the spots where Stu and Cissy always sat. On top of the kitchen bar were at least fifteen framed photographs of various grandchildren, nieces, and nephews. Most of the frames had brass curlicues looping around their perimeters. The small dark room was filled with homemade doilies, boxes of Kleenex, Cissy's knitting needles and Stu's fishing lures. This is where they'd decided to grow old together.

Before stopping by, Chief had taken us to study the trailer that Stu had up for sale. It was parked a few blocks away. We'd tried all the switches, got the AC going, pulled the blinds up and let them down again. We'd seen that you had to run the appliances with gas when you couldn't hitch up to a 110-volt outlet. We'd turned the pump on, flushed the toilet.

"Why was there water on the carpet?" Willy was now asking Stu at the dinette.

"Well," Stu said, then crossed his arms over his chest, preparing to tell the story. When you're in your twilight years, you make the most out of everything, even a small story. Willy and I understand this better than Stu suspected.

Stu is almost square, he's so short and fat. Like Willy's dad, he prefers not to wear his teeth because they're uncomfortable. Cissy returned to her spot across from the television. Both her La-Z-Boy and Stu's had bath towels on the seats, hand towels on the backs, wash cloths on the arm rests to prevent the chairs from wearing out too quickly. They would like the chairs to outlive them.

The Chief was on his third beer of the six-pack he asked us to buy him when we were getting sodas at the 7-11. He'd already had a little something before we picked him up.

The Chief has been known to cut a deal now and then, especially since he's living on virtually nothing but Social Security these days. Social Security off a social security number based on a card he got when he joined the navy at sixteen, over fifty years ago. He knows something's wrong with Willy's health, that my health is fine. He knows Willy's terminally ill, but Willy won't tell him exactly what it is.

The Chief was so excited that Willy and I might buy the trailer that we were perplexed. Maybe it was the beer talking. Or he wanted Willy and me to have at least a brief taste of the happiness he and his late wife shared for decades in trailers before our life together is over.

Maybe Stu was giving the Chief a kickback.

"Well," Stu said again, after thinking things over, "the reason there's water on the floor is because we had the trailer over to the beach." Now Stu tamped another cigarette on the dinette, lighted it. "Had to warsh the carpet. Still a little damp."

"Something's funny about the way the paneling's attached," Willy said. "It's all flimsy. You can see daylight everywhere."

"Boy hasn't spent enough time in trailers," Chief told Stu. "Don't know how they're rigged." The beer had made him frisky. At six foot three and two hundred fifty pounds, this was a lot of friskiness. You could land a fighter plane on the Chief's gray flat top.

Stu took everything under consideration, nodding, then said, "There was a fire in the trailer. Gutted it. Rebuilt it myself."

"I knew something was funny," Willy said. "That explains everything. The price . . ."

"First I heard of it," Chief said, his thick arms up in the air, Scout's honor. While they were up there, he cracked a fourth beer. "Ain't heard a word about it till now." Then he turned to me, said, "Don't know why I'm doing this, babe," meaning drinking the beer, "ain't had a drop in six months."

I asked Cissy if I could use the bathroom. It was Cissy's job to make guests comfortable, Stu's to tend to the finances.

"Oh, here—let me get rid of some of these," she said. She walked ahead of me to the bathroom, picking up damp towels left to dry on doorknobs.

"Don't know what we'd do around here without doorknobs," she said.

In the outer room I could hear Willy asking, "Can we go over and take another look?"

Stu grumbled, "So you think it's the type of thing you might want to buy?"

"I might," Willy said.

"Well, then, I *might* go over with you to look at it."

Stu and the Chief erupted in guffaws, knee slaps.

In the bathroom was a collection of porcelain figurines. My favorite was an elderly basset and schnauzer couple. She was wearing a poodle skirt and a bow, he a top hat and trousers. Like Stu and his wife, this couple had been together forever. They knew each other's imperfections and accepted them. They knew each other inside out.

So then Stu, the Chief, Willy, and I went over to inspect the trailer together. I suspect Cissy rarely leaves their mobile home. Stu and the Chief rode in one truck, Willy and I in another. Maybe Stu and the Chief talked about the length of Willy's sandy-blond hair during the ride. Willy's grown it out shoulder length, the longest it's ever been, like he doesn't have a care in the world. Or maybe the Chief and Stu listened to the CB radio, like they still do. I sat right next to Willy on the way over, our thighs touching. Later, I don't want to remember times we could have been closer, things I should have said.

Willy mumbled several times in different ways: "I *knew* there was something funny about that trailer. A fire . . . that explains some things . . ."

We got down on our hands and knees outside of the trailer. Stu's knees cracked like cap guns, his gut so big he could hardly show us how to light the gas. "You hear that?" he said when he'd lit the pilot and we heard a steady hissing. Willy and I nodded.

Stu showed us how to dump our gray water, our black water, how to make sure we were level, how to hitch the truck.

"You kids'll have so much fun," the Chief said. "Now lookit this here, babe," he said to me. His arm looped over my shoulder while he opened the trailer's bathroom door with the other. Inside, wallpaper made to look like wood paneling covered the particle board. He waved his arm inside as if it were door number three and a grand prize and not a three-foot-by-three-foot toilet and shower stall that smelled a little funky. "Ain't that something?" he said. He didn't know that it was Willy and not me, the woman, who wanted, needed, the bathroom. Either because of Willy's clothes or because of not being able to bear knowing, the Chief doesn't see that Willy is losing weight as a dozen smaller maladies and a few larger ones converge on his body.

I just know Stu must have thought us a couple of whippersnapper young kids to be buying a trailer in the first place, whippersnapper young kids who could afford to lose a little money on the deal. Even though we are family to Chief, I'm sure it was very clear to Stu and Cissy that they would never see us again.

On the drive home Willy pulled me towards him, our thighs again conjoined, said, "I wish I was going to be around to see *your* hair when it's gray and up in a little bun like Cissy's."

"Maybe you will be." My eyes filled, and I couldn't stand to look at him.

"I wish I was going to see you in bifocals and stretch pants and with Kleenex tucked in your watchband."

Willy is backing the trailer onto the side of our house. Stu drove it to Chula Vista earlier today, left it at a mobile home service center where Willy had a tow package attached to his truck so he could drive it home.

"You know what Stu did?" Willy asked a while ago. "Switched batteries on us. There was a perfectly good RV battery in it the other day. Now there's only a dead car battery."

At least we know the Chief hasn't been gossiping about Willy. Nobody, not even Stu, wants to think of himself as someone who cheats a sick person.

I'm standing in the street as we back the thing in for the first time so we'll be all ready for the trip in the morning. Willy wants me to watch cars coming from the south as he backs into the driveway. He wants me to watch cars coming from the north. He wants me to tell him which way to turn the wheel so he'll back in straight. He wants me to watch the trailer hitch and ball to make sure it doesn't hit the truck. He wants me to watch the tires so they don't run over the curb.

"I can't do all these things at the same time!" I scream at him.

My voice resonates in the air between us. I hear it over and over again. I'm sure I'll hear it later, too, when this is all over. Why do I have to be so loud? What's the matter with me?

"Try to be patient," he calls from the cab of the truck.

"But you're asking me to do something that's impossible." Of course I should be patient. Of course I should try.

"Just help me. Please."

And then he's holding me in his arms right out there on the curb. I see Archie, our tall, thin neighbor with the red ponytail from a few doors down, making his way over to help. Lately, he's been coming over more frequently. It started after my episode at the anniversary party, when I shouted out that Willy was sick. Archie was good about it, seemed to know more about it than what I was willing to say, waited for Willy to tell him himself. Once Willy did, Archie told us he had friends who'd died of AIDS. When he wanted to know what we were doing for protection, Willy told him the truth about that, too. The AIDS project downtown advised at the beginning that we use two condoms to be especially safe until it was discovered that two are actually more dangerous since they rub against each other and tear. Once we got through the first year of horror without having sex at all, we went back to using a single condom. The experts still don't understand why some get it and others don't, how I could have lived with Willy for several years and not contracted it myself.

Archie helps us maneuver the trailer into our driveway. Afterward I stand back and view it, freshly painted blue and white, hovering behind the idling truck. Maybe it will be good for us.

"Call Rosemary. See if she wants to go," Willy says. "It'll be fun."

I leave a message on Rosemary's voicemail. Rosemary is an old friend of mine, now a friend of ours, who was my roommate when I met Willy.

"So did you call her, hon?" Willy asks later. He messes up my hair, gives me a kiss. Tall and lanky, he has on his most recent pair of shockingly expensive tennis shoes, which he bought over a year ago and which are now held together with silver electrician's tape. He doesn't mind spending money occasionally, but he hates shopping, staying still long enough to try things on.

"You call her. It'll mean more to her if you leave a message," I tell him.

So Willy, too, leaves a message. "She *begged* me to call," he says on Rosemary's voice mail. We're laughing and he's staving off my hands, which are trying to grab the cell. "She begged me and is twisting my arm behind me at this very moment. Oh, it will be *so* much fun if you come, Rosemary. You're always *so* joyful to be around. We're going all the way up to San Onofre," he says before hanging up, "just to try everything out."

Later Rosemary calls back. Unlike the Chief, Rosemary knows exactly what is wrong. She knows because I told her. She and Willy have never discussed the issue outright, although he knows she knows and she knows he knows she knows. Willy doesn't want everyone to be aware of his sickness. Then they'll feel sorry for him and be careful around him and so his life will be over even sooner. Telling people is one of the things Willy and I clash on: the dangers of revealing it versus the dangers of keeping it all inside. At least Rosemary doesn't ask why we don't have children like so many other people think it's okay to ask.

Back on the cell, she says, "So, what, did you pin him against the wall or something to make him call me?" I can tell from the tone of her voice that aside from wanting to come, she thinks she *should* come, and always present in her voice now is the worry that if she doesn't come there may not be a next time. He could live six months. He could live three years.

"He begged me, really," I tell her, feeling a little desperate for her company.

But Rosemary already has plans with her new boyfriend. "Steve and I'll drive down in the morning, though. We'll go for a walk on the beach with you."

"Good," I say. "Great."

❖   ❖   ❖

Willy backs his truck up to the trailer the next morning for
our trip and I yell instructions. This time we handle the RV
like old pros.

We're on the road. Fifty miles from North Park to San Onofre.
The dog is in the back seat. The trailer seems to be going up and
down over invisible bubbles. We shimmy from side to side. Every
time a semi goes by the force of its wake makes us veer to the left.

"Are we almost there yet?" I ask.

"Only forty more miles."

Both of us adore the dog. Each of us sneaks him treats when
the other isn't looking. We call him sickeningly sweet love names.
The other night I found the two of them hugging in the pantry,
our baby's big red tail thumping against the washing machine.
"The two of you are going to have to take care of each other,
pal," Willy told the fluffy red ear while the dog eagerly licked at
his neck.

"There's the boobs," I say forty-five minutes later, spotting
them on the horizon.

And then, a while later, I tell him, "Did you hear about the kid,
Sean, going missing in the neighborhood?"

"One of the skateboarders?"

I nod. "According to his mother, Sabrina, he went to the beach
over a weekend and never came back. She's sick with worry."

Willy shakes his head.

We pull off the freeway onto the San Onofre exit. The ranger
Willy talked to on the phone said there was a one-mile walk to the
beach, that dogs were allowed, that we'd be staying in the San
Mateo section of the campground. All of it sounds perfect.

We're gazing over the Pacific as we take our turn driving up to
the ranger's booth. A handmade sign reads: *San Onofre is booked
solid. There are no vacancies.*

We tell the ranger our name.

"Don't see it here," she says.

"I've got a receipt," says Willy, reaching into his back pocket.

"You must be staying over in the San Mateo area or something," she says.

"Yeah, that's it."

She shakes her head, points down the road we just came in on. "You gotta go back, get on the freeway again, exit at Cristianitos and take a right, go onto the Camp Pendleton Marine Base, and you'll see it a half a mile up."

"Shit," Willy says, slamming his hand on the dashboard. "It's not on the beach?"

"We'll have fun anyway, honey," I tell him. "It'll be okay."

"I just can't believe it," Willy says. "No wonder there were campsites available in the summer. Who'd want to stay there?"

"It's better if you don't stress out, Willy. You want me to drive?" I shake my head and look away from him. "Just our luck," I say.

The ranger is a big woman. She adjusts the belt on her uniform, says: "Sorry, sir—go ahead and write a letter complaining. There's nothing I can do about it. We're all full up."

We manage to get the trailer turned around, follow the ranger's directions. There is no discussion of going home. Our life seems fated at this point, our destiny out of our hands. The radioactive boobs loom over everything we do.

Soon we're exiting the freeway at the other off ramp, heading onto the military base. I look down to the bottom of a dry, dusty canyon, see dozens and dozens of campers wedged compactly together—no trees, no lakes, no streams, nothing but dust.

"Can that really be it?" I say to Willy. "Would somebody stay here on purpose?"

I make a face when Willy looks at me, and somehow we both manage to laugh.

"I can't understand why they'd let people stay on a military base."

We pull in. The place is swarming with teenagers wearing lots of makeup, college couples who rarely peek out of tents. There are kids riding bikes everywhere.

"We're only here for one night, sweetheart," I say, laughing and patting Willy's leg.

At this ranger's window, there is a handwritten sign reading: *Mountain Lion seen in the area. Watch your children and pets.*

"Great," Willy says, "that'll just make our vacation complete."

I ask the ranger whether there are really mountain lions around here, while he looks on a chart for our reservation.

"A little girl got killed in June, but it was further up in the hills, different campground."

"Great," I say.

"There aren't mountain lions here," Willy says. "Too many people."

The ranger shakes his head. "Somebody reported one."

"One person?" Willy says.

Now the ranger nods. "*I* haven't seen a mountain lion, and I'm here every day. It was probably just a bobcat."

"Great," I say.

There is a crop of tomatoes or some other low-to-the-ground vegetable further down the dusty valley and covered with plastic. From a distance you can see the reflection off the plastic, pretend it is a lake that you are camping nearby. We drive up and down the campground lanes, amazed at how many people have been pushed together in one small area.

"Who would intentionally camp here?" I ask Willy.

Willy shrugs. "It's cheap and near the beach."

I nod as we go down another lane, this one full of loud rock music.

"Great," Willy says.

When we find lot 81, we back the trailer in without a problem. Not only are we not at the beach, but we are in a handicapped spot adjoining the public restrooms. Men, women, and children from all over the grounds cut the corners of our lot walking through to use the john, rinse their dirty dishes, brush their teeth.

"Great," Willy and I say at different times. We pat each other's knees.

I let the dog out of the truck. Immediately he runs to the campground two feet from ours. I watch as a family of five pet him, say how pretty he is. Then the dog runs into their tent, comes out with a package of Oreos.

"I'm so sorry," I say.

Even at home our house is further from our neighbors'. It's as if everyone has decided to pitch a tent on the freeway. The only thing to do at the bottom of this mostly barren, unlandscaped canyon is observe one another.

I tie the dog up. He gets more room in our backyard.

"The refrigerator won't light," Willy says. We can't use electrical here since there aren't any hookups. Willy rushes to one side of the trailer, then to the other. Wherever I go, whatever I try to do, I am in his way. Soon he will have our whole trip planned out: hiking, singing by the fire, fishing if there is any. Like with Stu and Cissy, our duties are clearly delineated: mine is to explode occasionally, let some of the steam off. Willy's is to keep us busy.

"I'm going to walk the dog up to the ranger's and make sure we can take him on the beach," I tell Willy, who is completely preoccupied with the trailer.

The dog and I walk the half mile up. Everywhere there are tents, so close they're almost touching. Is this what my life would have been like if I'd had children? Squalid living conditions, no privacy, a husband with a buzz cut who squashed beer cans in his fist?

There is one concrete bathroom after another all the way up the hill. You have to figure that a hundred people must be assigned to each one. A serial killer could easily pretend he's taking a stroll at 3:00 a.m. when momentarily you're the only one using the toilet. Or he could hide in one of the stalls and wait. Or camp next door and conceal the bodies in his tent.

The ranger explains two trails the dog can go on. He pets the dog, says he's a good boy.

"I think the refrigerator's broken," Willy says when I get back.

He can't fix things like refrigerators at home. I don't know why he thinks he can fix one here. "Give it a little time," I tell him. "Stu said you had to give it some time."

"Stu said he was selling us a new battery."

"It's just a battery, honey," I say, but I'm wondering if buying the trailer might have been a mistake. Maybe we're in over our heads.

I look up at a tall concrete post on our campsite. There seem to be speakers coming out of the top. "What's this?" I ask Willy.

"Sirens."

"What do you mean?"

"Nuclear plants have to install sirens within so many miles in case there's a meltdown."

I sigh.

I follow Willy around outside of the trailer as he listens to the different pilot lights, but I can't stop glancing at the siren and wondering why it has to be on our lot, why it has to be us.

Inside the trailer I try to put things away, to retrieve chairs, but as soon as I do, Willy's on his knees in front of the refrigerator again, feeling the racks for coolness, blocking the way.

I tell him, "I'm going to call Rosemary so she doesn't go to the wrong campground."

But when I try the cell, I discover we're between towers. "I'll see if there's a pay phone."

Once I've walked back to the station, the ranger explains there are no pay phones on the campgrounds. The closest one is at a Carl's Jr., about a two-hour walk. "Good boy," he says to my dog, who loves everybody.

"Two hours round trip," Willy asks back at our site, "or two hours each way?"

I shrug, tell him I could walk back and ask, but he shakes his head. "Let's just unhook the trailer and drive the truck over."

"You don't want to do all that, Willy. You'll be exhausted."

Willy's hands are on his hips, and he's perspiring. He's shrinking before my eyes. Yes, we should never have bought the trailer. It was silly to believe the trips it took us on could help us have a life like Stu and Cissy's. We've thrown away money we're going to need for more important things—the medications, the hospitals, after that.

It's hard to imagine how important a link the Chief might be for me when these things start happening, the Chief, who has certainly been known to get on my nerves, and I on his. His enthusiasm over the trailer must have been his shared excitement over future camping trips. Since the beginning, the three of us have camped together, before we got married, before this disease. We'd fish, throw sticks into the lake for the dog, sing along with Willy's guitar in the evening. Later, after I'd crawled into the tent to sleep, the two of them would get into the apricot brandy and sing "Jack Was a Lonesome Cowboy" and "They Had to Carry Harry to the Ferry." This was back when their bodies could afford pints of apricot brandy, when I had a day to throw away for pouting over their keeping me awake.

Willy looks away from our campsite, says, "Well, after dinner we'll walk a little ways, see how far the Carl's Jr. is. How do you get there?"

"He said you take the dirt path by the regular road," I say, pointing.

"We have to be careful—I heard what sounded like marines practicing artillery up there."

I sigh.

Willy smiles, then shakes his head again. "Damn refrigerator," he says.

"It's only a refrigerator. You can ask Andy about it when we get back."

Willy won't tell Andy, his brother, what he has either. Willy won't tell anyone. I don't know what he does with the information. I, of all people, was the one that had to be admitted to the hospital because I couldn't stand the thoughts in my head anymore. I can't stand to think of what it will be like afterward. In my mind there is a black hole.

"How can you not think about it?" I finally asked him after I was admitted.

"I'm always thinking about it. It's always on my mind."

Only I have told people, have had to tell people. Otherwise I can't seem to function. So, no, Andy, a little on the old boy side like the Chief, hasn't been told exactly what his brother Willy has. But, of course, because of the very fact that Willy won't say, what else can it be?

We're eating steaks Willy has barbecued. It's getting dark. The trailer is between where we're sitting by a fire and the public restrooms. Occasionally people walk through our lot, toilet paper and mess kits in tow. Across the lane are two families with two adult couples, two teenage girls wearing lots of lipstick and eye shadow and interested in the college boys on the other side of the restrooms, and next to us is the family with the cookies. Every once in a while one of them calls our dog's name and throws another Oreo. Willy and I can't figure out how the five of them fit all their stuff into one car, what with a large tent, clothes, sleeping bags, and a surfboard.

I do the dishes after dinner, straighten things up. The cell phone still doesn't work.

We're walking up the hill towards the Carl's Jr. Maybe the phone will perk up at the top of the hill with fewer obstructions. The dog is on a leash.

Willy laughs at me. "Come on," he says as we climb the paved hill. Cars shoot past us, spraying gravel, blinding us with their brights because they can't figure out who would be out on such a busy highway at this time of night. He puts his arm around me, points out the dirt path only twenty feet away. We both know it's there. "Let's walk on the dirt. There aren't any mountain lions."

"I'm sorry, Willy. You just have to accept this about me. I can't do it. I won't walk there. I'm positive there are ten or twenty mountain lions just waiting for us to step off the road." Partly I'm laughing, partly I'm not.

Willy hits his forehead with the palm of his hand. "Honey, there hasn't been a mountain lion here in thirty years. You heard the ranger."

"What's the difference between a mountain lion and a bobcat?"

"If a bobcat saw us, he'd run *away* from us. They only weigh thirty pounds. A mountain lion weighs a hundred and forty, and he'd run *for* us."

"Please, Willy, I can't."

"Fine." He reaches his arms up in the air in exasperation.

I lean over to the dog, say, "I don't want my little sweetie to get eaten." Every time I talk baby talk, the dog wags his tail. A civilized animal, he's more terrified by the headlights than we are. He wouldn't do well with a bobcat.

Above us, the radioactive boobs flicker with red lights telling airplanes and everyone else to stay away.

We're leaning against a guard rail trying again to call Rosemary. The rail doesn't seem like a safe place to be, such a thin piece of metal to do such a big job. What I don't mention to Willy is how afraid I am of who's inside those cars. All those serial killers not yet caught have to get around somehow. They have to drive cars too. Who's to say they don't travel this road, that a serial killer doesn't live in the neighborhood? They have to live somewhere. There's nothing ridiculous about this, I want to tell Willy. Just watch the news at night. What he doesn't understand is how it all builds up inside me, takes on a life of its own, how I can't sleep at night with all this danger going on.

The cell phone screen lights up, and when I punch in the numbers we hear beeping sounds, but all we keep getting is a busy signal.

More cars come flying around the corner and then swerve, not knowing who or what we are, sitting here with a phone screen with green lights, and a frightened dog on our leash on the shoulder of a busy highway. I ask Willy: "Is that a tract development?"

We look out across the valley where the campground is, over to another hill. Willy nods. The usual Friday night traffic has picked up on Interstate 5 between San Diego and Los Angeles, making so much noise it's hard to do much else besides nod. While most of the hills and mountains in the area are barren, the one across the way is densely populated with what looks like near-identical houses and street lamps a near-identical number of yards apart.

A car comes over the hill so fast it almost loses control, so I agree to take the dirt path back to our campsite, despite the mountain lions. When we arrive at the trailer, Willy says, "There's water on the carpet exactly where it was that first day."

"You're kidding." We're on our hands and knees again, touching it, smelling it. "It must be from when I did the dishes," I say. "It must have come through the floor."

"Great," Willy says, shaking his head. "Can you believe it? Stu out and out lied."

Now we're sitting in our chairs outside by the fire. I scoot mine over, right next to Willy's, pat his knee. "It's only a trailer," I tell him. "Just a trailer."

I think about Stu and Cissy watching cartoons on their bath towels, Stu and Cissy with whom we have more in common than any of the young families camping or in the tracts above us, and I wonder how they're able to rationalize such things. They must think a little lie is okay because they are the ones in their golden years, because they are the ones who have put in hard lives and now deserve to relax as they creep closer to whatever they believe happens afterward. And then I feel sorry for them because they don't know Willy like I do, because they don't know what a horrible waste this is. They can't possibly comprehend what's really happening. Who knows what happens next? Maybe eventually, in some other life, they will discover the truth, after all. And maybe the truth will seem like nothing in the bigger picture.

We're sitting by our siren and looking up at the stars above the valley. It's a clear night, and there are stars everywhere. I gaze at them, then over at Willy looking at them, then back to the stars. He has questions about destiny, about what happens next, whether there really are such places as heaven and hell, things a thirty-nine-year-old man should be able to laugh off. There isn't anything I can do, even imagine what he must think about tomorrow or the next day. Heaven and hell are as real to me as a man sitting on a cloud and calling himself God.

I hold his hand, and we peer over at the campsite next to us. "Are they all sleeping in the one tent?" Willy whispers. I shrug, but we figure they must be. How do they all fit?

We watch the kids playing across the lane, kids we will never have. They ride their bikes, push the brakes as hard as they will go, competing to see who can leave the longest skid mark. One of the fathers comes out. All the adults have been playing poker. This dad says, "I told you not to ride those bikes anymore. That's it. Wash your faces and then you're in the camper. Got it? No bikes tomorrow."

"*Dad.*"

"We'll see . . . if you get in bed *now.*"

The boys scurry across our lot with their toothbrushes as fast as they can to the public sink. We smile as they whisper to each other to hurry up, hurry up or they'll have to *walk* to the beach tomorrow.

"So you think they'll ever really use them?" I ask Willy, patting the concrete base that leads up to the nuclear siren.

"Sure," he says. "We're using more and more of that energy."

"Soon?"

"It's inevitable."

Families in the subdivision above us settle down to relax for the evening, too. Homely blue and white lights flicker across their windows and down into the valley, onto us.

I tell Willy, "I bet Rosemary's sorry she's missing this—nestled in on the military base on our relaxing camping trip . . ."

". . . with our phone that doesn't work," he adds.

". . . or we'd be calling Stu and telling him a thing or two." Not to mention feeling reassured we could call out if we ran into a mountain lion, or the next serial killer.

That's when we hear what sounds like a piece of metal clanking loudly behind us—a shrill, piercing sound, it whines, crashes, clangs. It reverberates throughout the whole trailer, onto the pavement, through our feet, screaming in the air around us.

"*What?*" I shriek. "*What?*" I jump to my feet, knock over my chair.

The Oreo family unzips and peeks out of their tent. The boys across the way, finally in bed, crack the curtains of the camper.

"It's the siren!" I shout. "*Oh my God, it's the siren!*"

My hands are on my face and I can hardly believe it—is

everyone running out of their campsites, towards us? Are we really having a catastrophe?

Stunned, Willy finally reacts. He moves close, one of my shoulders in each of his hands. "I think it's just the water pump, honey," he says, though he too looks scared. "It's just the trailer."

"It's just a trailer," I say, but now I can't stop crying.

The dog barks and runs into the tent next door, as Willy and I turn to face the rest of the world. We gaze up at the siren, beyond.

Crickets are somehow cricking, though there's hardly any ground cover in this place for them to hide in. The stars are so thick and full, twinkling, throbbing, falling—all at the same time—so beautiful over all of us, this ugly and overfull population, that they make you think there must be some reason we're here, wedged in together. They make you focus out there, project yourself, airborne, slithering with the comets, the constellations, the galaxies, somewhere out there where we all come from, where I have to believe we'll see each other again.

Dear Sam,

Edgar here, from the old neighborhood. I can't stop eyeballing the TV, searching for some kind of answer. My body feels about dead on the couch. We've had another plane crash in San Diego, and it's all over the news. Not right here in North Park but a few miles up the coast. Close enough it's hard to stomach after what we went through in '78. I don't want it in my head anymore, but I can't stop watching.

I got your new address a few years ago from Mrs. Jawarski down at Jubilee Seniors, where she's staying now. I've been meaning to write, but can't seem to sit down and do it. Guess it's always the ladies who keep track of these things. You probably heard Betty passed on. I'm alone now.

I really need to talk to you, buddy. Nobody else understands what we went through back then. The folks living here now had some kind of party on the thirtieth anniversary, but they don't know, not really. Couldn't go myself since the leg was acting up. Couldn't even get into the wheelchair. They invited me, though.

Now the news is showing two homes burning up as I write this. North of here. Military jet. The houses are all but gone as I watch. I can't seem to get up or out of my slippers since I saw the black smoke out the window and turned on the tube. Couldn't go to work today. They keep playing the same segments again and again, plain as day. It's all too much.

I got myself a part-time job at the gas station by Dwight and 32nd. A couple of times a week I go in and sell gas and a few candy bars while the guys take lunch.

The family up in University City is crying on the TV and trying to get past the police tape to see if their loved ones are alive. It's all happening right in front of me as I stare at the set in the same old two-bedroom bungalow I always lived in. Remember the cactus out front? It's about twelve feet tall these days. A baby and two ladies killed right in their home. You'd think I'd have all this stuff figured out by now, why some people get picked and not others. People are running to get away from the burning gas and fumes, getting into vans and rushing for the freeway.

You remember the refrigerated vans all over the neighborhood, don't you, bud? The SWAT team picking up body parts, throwing them inside? Endless sirens. You remember not knowing when it's safe to go back. I'm not sure it's ever safe, Sam. No matter where you go.

University City grew out of nowhere around the time you left and all those people started emptying out of the Midwest and coming this way and needing a place to stay. Course, they had no idea this would happen.

Korean fellow, husband and father of the ones that were killed, comes out on the news a little bit ago and says we got to pray for the pilot who parachuted so he doesn't suffer. Says it wasn't the pilot's fault. Damnedest thing.

You spend your life hoping the dangerous parts are over, but never quite believe it. When Betty gave me the slippers just before she went on, they made me feel safer. Still do, no matter how old. I wouldn't tell most people that. Or the part about never getting out of my sweat pants today, into respectable trousers and a work shirt. First, all the clean ones are in a heap in the bedroom. The kids say I should get someone to help, but what do they know, living all over the country like they do? I haven't seen the bottom of that pile too many times since Betty passed.

Scary, ain't it? Remembering the day the Boeing hit? Everywhere you looked legs were hanging off fences and phone wires and acacia trees. The Shermans' old cocker spaniel died on the front yard, and that was it. Betty couldn't stop crying. I don't blame you a bit for moving on after what it did to your house, Sam. Not after the place boomed and lit up like World War II. Sometimes I wish I could get out of here, too. The older folks are mostly gone now—either to homes, like Milly Jawarski, or in with their kids. I figured I may as well stay here and dare the gods. If you can get singled out once by a 727, you can get singled out again no matter where you are. But the neighborhood doesn't feel safe, no. Sometimes I think I can still smell flesh burning.

Yeah, the younger folks have moved in and taken over. Bright colored houses instead of all the little white bungalows like it used to be. Probably got more of those parrots than we used to. Mostly I wish they'd stay away because of all the spots they leave on the house, but I got a turquoise one that likes to collect himself on the neighbor's roof when I'm sitting on the front porch. We keep an eye on things. The kids grow plants now that don't need water since they say we're living in a desert here and shouldn't waste the resources. You ask me, it's not a waste to have a little greenery around. I miss the old Italian Cypresses and weeping willows.

The neighbors take out the aerial photos that got took all those years ago, right after the crash, and think they can imagine, but they can't. What do they know about friends and neighbors losing their homes in a second? Some of us are just plain cursed. They're okay, though, these new kids. Ask me how I'm doing when I can get out of the house.

Albert's still down at the corner. I see an old Mexican gal pushing his wheelchair through the neighborhood, and I try to get out and wave, but I'm not sure he knows it's me anymore. I'd go on over and tell him about this current situation if I could just get myself out of the house.

But I don't blame you, Sam. Really I don't. I might leave here too if I had anywhere to go.

Just thought you might want to know.

Regards,

Edgar

Nimbus Cumulus

We lie cushioned in sour grass and sticky sweet pine needles at the base of the canyon. Clouds pass over, and I tell Wes they look like sunflowers, convertible automobiles, the Eiffel Tower. He says nothing, so I tell him to try, and he says one looks like a recital hall. I groan."Nimbus Cumulus!" I say.

"Huh?"

"We can call the dog Nimbus Cumulus since he's so dark and dramatic."

"Whatever."

Lights in the hill wink on simultaneously, as if centrally controlled. We walk quietly up the hill to the trailer, hoping to avoid our neighbors.

I get the dog in our temporary home here in the small town of Hemet, ninety minutes up the coast, this first time we leave the city and North Park. Wes and I need a distraction, something we can care for. His rage has become uncontrollable. Back in North Park, where we live most of the time, Lenora has just recently bought the house across the street , and we know most of the rest of the neighbors at least to say hello to. People tend not to leave once they're there.

Nimbus is huge, part of a big litter, and bullied his twin sister called Neophobia—fear of the new. Even so, they're inseparable. When Wes and I first split them up, they would run away to be together.

Wes thinks the dog looks like a vulture because of his hook nose. He's a silly-looking mutt: part shepherd, part husky and, the owners swore, part coyote, though I think this was only a selling point. Sometimes he seems awfully stupid, like when he yelps and drools at the sliding glass door. Other times he's unusually smart.

The trailer we rent on the outskirts of Hemet cramps us from the start. We try to ignore that it's the smallest place we've lived since marrying six years ago. We overlook that stray arms and legs on our clothes face amputation every time we close the broom closet, that we have to take showers in the park bathroom because sheets of music have overtaken our Plexiglas stall, that we have to grocery shop every night since the cupboards are full of possessions we can't part with. We use decorations from our small home in North Park, now rented out, hang prints on the ceiling, arrange a wooden crate with a pillow and blanket on the patio for Nimbus Cumulus.

On the only unoccupied corner of the bed, Wes shoves his trombone out of the way, and we squeeze close and eat tuna sandwiches. He stands and belches and nods his head with the radio. "Let's get rid of Lauren," he says, tossing a fork into the aluminum sink.

"What do you mean?" I unzip my boots, let them fall to the floor.

"*Everything.*" His dark eyes are as wild as the day I met him at Windansea Beach in La Jolla. He thrusts open the door and hurls his tuna fish salad plate. So I throw out the electric blanket his mother gave him for graduation in 1994, and he throws out my schefflera plant, and I throw out my art history textbooks. The woman in the next trailer closes her door and peers out the window. We sit and pant for a minute, giggling. Then Wes grabs my arm and tries, unsuccessfully, to drag me out the door. With little resistance, I pull off his jeans, toss them onto the counter. We make love on the dinette while Nimbus Cumulus thumps his tail in time and barks jealously. We hear only crickets.

❖ ❖ ❖

Just after we got married, when I moved in with him to the house he'd grown up in in North Park, Wes came to every single one of my performances, brought bouquets of California poppies and primrose, wildflowers like sage and buckwheat, whether I danced lead or in the corps. I did pirouettes for him in public, next to the fountain in Balboa Park, both of us giggling and bumping into each other. Sometimes at home we made love while I wore a tutu and toe shoes. Happy to live so close to downtown where we both went for performances, we walked the neighborhood, asked neighbors about their plants, went home with cuttings, admired the Mexican tile on their steps. A handful of neighbors knew him as a boy, loved him back then and love him still. They've listened to him practice his trombone all these years. Now he's something of local legend since he lived here at the time of the crash. I get tired of it coming up so often. Why dwell? What the locals never see are the times when this passionate man breaks and goes on self-destruct.

A couple of years after moving into the neighborhood, disquieted by his not winning a seat in the symphony, we huddled in bed, his breath on my collarbone, my elbow braced on his shoulder, vaguely attached to the hand involved in his hair, his crinkled knee nestled in the softness of my behind, and we heard noises on our generally quiet block. Young men from the old apartment building used the street as a stage for unaudienced soliloquies, couples of women platform-heeled it home from barroom sojourns, Trans Ams from rougher neighborhoods nearby backfired into the night while unexplained voices screamed. We tried not to hear.

Often, when I got home from rehearsal, Wes was still awake. "If I don't get some sleep," he'd say, "I'm not even going to bother with the audition."

"How many days until the next one?" I'd say and warm some milk.

I did ballet stretches first thing in the morning to relax after those restless nights and punched in during the day as a telephone operator. Wes blew his nose, stood under the shower, played scales on the trombone, and watched *Roadrunner*. He worked for Tiny at Tiny's Towing, from 12 to 12, three days a week.

At Sprint, I sat in a row of women wearing earpieces in front of big screens. I made overseas connections, occasional telephonic jokes, broke in for emergencies and wondered who those people in my mouthpiece were. At lunch, I brown bagged it with girls right out of high school, girls still dreamy about love who spoke with unweighted energy about affairs that popped up and were just as easily discarded, girls for whom better things were right around the corner. The older women's jobs weren't so temporary. I avoided them.

Sometimes I lunched with Chelsea, who danced with me at Alice Matthews' Experimental Theatre. She was tall and thin and had an ocean of black hair that crashed like waves on her shoulders. When her first husband left her, she had a red rose tattooed over her left hip "because I knew things had to get better."

"Have they?" I once asked her.

"I tell them from the very start they can take a hike if they aren't going to treat me right. Fuck 'em if they can't take a joke."

Chelsea often spent the night with us during rehearsal schedule instead of commuting. Wes thought she was hard; she thought he was macho. He let her stay, though. We knew she was lonely. He carried her overnight bag in for her, made sure the doors were locked, got her a drink.

Wes became buddies with Tiny at the tow company. Tiny was tiny and so was his wife, Ruby, except for huge thighs spread from years at the dispatcher's desk. They met in Provo. Wes adored the couple, saw them as marital role models. I liked the two regardless. Tiny had a tattoo of a snake wrapped around his left forearm from an old motorcycle club, the first car he ever towed on his right, a ship covering his entire back from the navy, and a ruby ring tattooed over his heart.

After two Budweisers, Ruby liked to tell the story of how Tiny and his baby blue convertible Chrysler had rolled into the truck stop where she was working in Provo.

"There I was waitin' on the same old crowd and in walks Raymond, spic'n'span in his black and whites. I loved that uniform . . ."

"Aw, Rube, they don't want to hear this crap," Tiny would say, his feet on the table and a smile as long as the highway out of a dry town in Utah.

"Well, I couldn't take my eyes off him and that convertible of his." She blushed when he brought out old pictures of her in the bubble bath with ribbons in her hair.

The first year Wes lost the audition for the San Diego Symphony, he crashed the new truck. Tiny realized Wes's talent despite the sharp edges, saw him as a son, and didn't fire him. I danced lead two nights in Los Angeles. Wes didn't come to watch. After that was when we moved to Hemet for six months, to get away from everything, to let Wes calm down.

In Hemet, soon after moving out of North Park this first time, I go to the neighbor lady's trailer to ask her about electric fixtures. She's curious and invites me in for coffee even though I have Nimbus with me.

"Our motors were wearing out," I explain, watching her fit a crisp filter into her Mr. Coffee. She keeps two small children in the trailer with her.

"Lot a folks move out here for a while, especially young ones. They always go back."

"We may, eventually." I don't like the way she wants us to fit as snugly as her trailer bed folds up and fits into the wall. I lean over and kiss Nimbus Cumulus on the snout.

"It's quiet out here," she says, setting a mug in front of me that says "Nan," then sitting.

"Yes, awfully quiet. I hope Wes's practicing doesn't bother you." I think about Nimbus Cumulus, too, howling when we put him out at night.

"Oh, no—I like hearing him. I used to play piano myself. As long as it's not too late. What's he in, some kind of rock-and-roll band?"

"He plays jazz now, but he's really a classical trombonist. He almost got into the San Diego Symphony." I haven't voiced the name of our nemesis in a while and think about the city more than I have since our move.

"I almost got the job playing piano at the church," Nan tells me. "But almost is almost."

"Oh, he's very good, though." I muse over our long walks downtown, past evening grocers, trying on clothes we can't afford at the Nordstrom's in Horton Plaza, the night we fought and the mime stalked Wes with an identical pout for half a block until he had to laugh.

"Because there's good and then there's *good*," Nan is saying. "You get caught up on good and you make a mess of things. Now you take Charlie and me. He only comes home for ten days of the month, at best. Rest of the time he's driving his rig. Now I could squawk and carry on, but I decided that's the way it is. No sense turning mean."

"The tension got us all locked up," I tell her. I remember Wes kicking the furniture, the holes he put in the walls, my leaving the house, fearful, driving.

"Sure it will. That city . . ." And then the phone rings, and I am glad to be able to motion good-bye while Nimbus and I slip through the gate adjoining our property.

I wind up with another phone job in Hemet, though I'd hoped this would change. The Y.M.C.A. is the only place that gives dance lessons. Wes takes a position in a government-sponsored C.E.T.A. band.

The difference between Wes and me is that I don't mind taking a break. He does. I believe this might be the difference between being competent and a true artist.

Chelsea calls me at the phone company on the free WATS line from where she works. She has taken a married lover in Coronado. They see each other twice a month. I doodle on the pink while-you-were-out pads and pretend to take messages.

"But, Chelsea," I whisper. "That's not very often. Do you like him very much?"

"No time with rehearsals anyway. Sure I like him. We stayed at the Hilton last night."

"God, I'd always think about him going home to his wife."

"It's better than being his wife. I get him when he wants to have fun, not when he wants to bitch and moan."

At the Y, we practice the same *tour jetés* and leaps and then wait for the ballet instructor to find a new record. She can't afford a pianist. We have a fast turnover of girls. They come to take off a few pounds.

"We played at a nut house today," Wes says. The unfinished cupboards jump with the impact of his case thrown on the dinette. Nimbus Cumulus darts out the door.

I slide over on the mustard vinyl seat, which is attached to the cupboards, which are attached to the sink.

"The only ones who applaud are the nurses and the shrinks. After Getz, some kid asked if we could play 'Achy Breaky Heart.' I mean, come on. Tomorrow's a nursing home, then an elementary school . . ." He slaps his hand on the shower stall. The trailer rocks like an amusement park ride. "I could go to take a crap in the morning and the floor might fall out!"

"Sure, let's knock out the dining room and install a sunken bathtub and a bidet . . ."

"Okay. Okay. But a trailer? We're on top of each other more than we want to be. And every time I sit outside that guy next door tells me where to get the best buy on butane."

"We're not going back until you calm down—it scares me."

"Forget what happened in the city," he says. "How can you stand living all crammed in here like this? I can't breathe."

"It's okay for a while. We're saving money."

"Do you have to be so goddamn reasonable?" he asks. I close my eyes and listen to the salt shaker tumble as his hand slams onto the counter. "Don't you ever get upset about *anything*?" The gravel stuck in the soles of his shoes crackles on the simulated wood floor. Sometimes I'm afraid he's right. Sometimes I'm afraid the only reason I stay is because he's one of the few people I know who fights so hard.

"I'm sorry. I can't stand myself when I do that," he says, when I return from taking Nimbus Cumulus for a walk. He concentrates on the dinette. "I'm going to replace this with wood over the weekend. I can't stand Formica. I'm trying."

I nod agreeably.

"Come here," he says. I step into his arms and we hug for a long time and he adds, "I don't know what I'd do without you."

When we let go, I look away from his distress at not being talented enough to make it, the part he doesn't want me to see. We tell each other how in love we are and talk about the possibilities of moving back. We're more careful the rest of the night.

The second year Wes loses out at the audition at the San Diego Symphony is worse. We haven't yet discussed trailer parks or Hemet this time, and it seems as though maybe we won't have to go, but then we do. With an air of finality, he snuggles the trombone into its bed of red velvet, snaps shut the brass fasteners and, as if bowling a sure strike, slides the case under the bed. Then he sits in the vinyl chair across from the TV in our little North Park bungalow for two weeks. He curls his bottom lip, cements his arms across his chest, seeds his feet, and waits for the cobwebs to grow.

I call Tiny, who sighs and says, "Sure, sure," and then I buy enough food at the bodega around the corner so that when I go to work Wes can eat without my knowing.

The lead solo falls ill, and I get the part. It's in the *Union-Tribune*, but I tell Wes the paper hasn't been delivered yet. He still isn't talking. I tell the girls at work, and they bring champagne, and we drink it at the boards and make off-tune comments to people trying to connect with nephews in Omaha. I stay late at rehearsals.

Wes is practicing when I come home one night. He blushes as if I've caught him with a lover, stands, holds me for a long time and tells me how much he loves me. He's cleaned the house and bought groceries. He grills chicken and vegetables on the backyard hibachi.

He goes back to work the next day, and I think everything will be okay. The city decides to tow away cars in Pacific Beach that aren't moved for street sweeping. At 6:45 a.m., when Tiny's and plenty of other trucks station themselves on Cass and Grand, where the street signs clearly say: "Monday Street Cleaning 7:00 a.m.–5:00 p.m.," Wes gets in a fight over a maroon Peugeot with Al from Al's.

"I was just about to sink my hooks in the bumper," Al tells Tiny on the radio. "It was 6:59, and this jackass backed right up to the trunk."

"The joker's got a Triple A sticker right on his bumper," is Wes's defense. "You carry National, not Triple A."

"This is city work, pal. We ain't working insurance. We're working city. Go check your manual or wax the truck or something. This one's mine."

Instead, Wes waxes Al's jaw and Al sinks his hooks into Wes's legs. Then Tiny drives up and orders Wes to take the red Toyota across the street and apologizes to Al. "The kid's a little emotional—he just lost out at the symphony."

"I don't care if his old man sings soprano," says Al. And then he lifts the maroon Peugeot and drives away. Wes starts playing jazz at a small club where he gets to know Cecil, an old sax player. Sometimes Wes and the others go over to Cecil's after work. They listen to Lester Young and the Duke, pass bottles of Jose Gold. He never quits practicing for the symphony though.

Wes also gets to know Rempt, a funny old guy new to the neighborhood. Rempt sells multi-colored crystals by the handful, gives Wes a clustered amethyst to help calm him.

"Now he's into oxygen," Wes tells me one day.

"What does he do with that?" I ask.

"I guess he breathes it . . ."

I roll my eyes. "Besides that."

"We had cranberry last night. I guess it's supposed to relax you."

Personally, I think the fact that this Rempt person is so offbeat is what makes Wes comfortable around him. Rempt is an old friend of Neil's and is trying to help Neil and Sabrina find their oldest boy. There's a rumor, though, that Sean has now met with and talked to his younger brother, Matt, but he still hasn't contacted his parents. Rempt's niece, Susan, hit it off with Sean right before he disappeared and is helping, too. Now when I look out the window, it's Susan skateboarding with Matt. Her natty long hair has turned into Rastafarian curls floating behind her, shapely, beautiful in its own way, though I don't know how she'll ever get a job or if she even wants one.

The reviewers don't like Alice Matthews' experimental choreography. "The creator of 'A Day in Julian' ought to pack a picnic and take a long waltz." They mention my lead, though, and several say I show promise. One complains, "She had the dance down technically, but refused to put any more of herself on the line." Chelsea sends a red rose. When I get home, Wes has fixed the coffeemaker and made chef's salad for two.

I consider not telling him about the review, but then don't.

"Why do you even bother living with me?" he says, ashamed of himself for not paying attention to my performance. He leaves for two hours without telling me where he's going, returns more peaceful, and that's when we agree to take another breather in Hemet. It isn't too long after Archie's anniversary party for the plane crash.

"I love you," Wes says. We go to bed early. Someone's car is broken into down the street that night. "One more year," he says

Once we're in Hemet, I still drive back to San Diego to see Chelsea and check the house in North Park. I see my good friend Annie who lives across the street from our place, too. Annie's husband has gotten worse, more opportunistic diseases. She's started having to tell her family what Willy has.

"We're getting along better," I tell my mother in the Claire de Lune Coffee Lounge where we have agreed to meet.

"I should hope so." My mother looks worn out, but then she's always looked worn out, long before she finished raising three kids and tending to the house all those years. Wes and I have been in Hemet six months. My parents have lived in the suburbs forever.

"He's not as bad as you and Dad choose to believe," I say, wishing I hadn't called them the night he threw his trombone case at me and then his trombone straight through the front window. No matter how much I vacuum, I still find shattered glass, and cut my foot just the other night.

"Being that angry can be dangerous," she says, sniffing, rubbing her napkin on the gold-speckled table in a spot the waitress has missed. She has a way of keeping things out of her psyche, like she wears a plastic shield. Maintaining order is the only job she's ever had as my father never wanted her to work. It's her way of refusing to feel anything even remotely painful, an anesthetization with its own dangerous side effects. "We worry, you know."

"He didn't mean to, Mother. You know that. I don't want to have to defend him every time I see you. You're not the one who married him. I don't know how you live with a man who hangs his tools in alphabetical order and folds his underwear before he puts them in the hamper." I stop myself and glance down at the napkin I've shredded.

Even though she wants to understand, my mother isn't taking this very well. "Do you still have that big dog in the trailer with you?" I nod while she unzips the side pocket of her imitation leather purse, pulls out a list on which I am one of many details in her life: *Weight Watchers, lunch 12:30, deposit checks, chuck roast, call IRS.*

"Does Wes like his new job?" Her voice is softer.

"Playing in a C.E.T.A. band for schools and hospitals isn't the route Coltrane took, but it's less stressful." Out the window, I watch pedestrians and cars tooling slowly down University Avenue, stopping to shop at small stores. I find myself missing the urban yet homey feel.

"I just want you to be happy," she says, while the register rings up our ticket. Carefully, she crosses out *lunch 12:30*. We look into each other's eyes, and the nod I direct to her probably has two very different meanings.

Sometimes Chelsea drives up to spend a weekend with us in Hemet. She's started growing on Wes. Sometimes Tiny and Ruby drive up, and we have dinner and play Canasta. Wes and Tiny argue over how many tons a truck would have to be to tow a trailer. After Ruby and I pump water and do the dishes, I curl up with Nimbus on the bed and grill Ruby to find out how she ever adjusted from Provo. Once, after drinking a half a pint of Scotch between them, Wes started teasing Tiny about the long lunch breaks he used to take.

"All for a good cause," beamed Tiny.

"Shush your mouth, Raymond," Ruby warned Tiny.

"Got some pretty good nooners in my day. Not so bad before breakfast neither."

"You stop it, Raymond. You and your drinking . . . makes me wish I'd never left Utah."

"Aw, heck, Rube. What would you do without me?"

We smirked and said we were going to walk over to the bathroom when Ruby told him she could have married Stanley Johnson who now owned a big farm in Logan.

But the times we're most content are on Sunday afternoons alone. Holding hands, we hike over to where the new freeway has just gone through. Wes races the dog to the construction site of the new Bank of America and Von's grocery store. Our neighbors think it will be very convenient when they do not have to drive all the way to town to buy a head of lettuce. It seems as if nothing will ever go wrong again.

The third year Wes loses the audition at the San Diego Symphony, I tell him we have to leave immediately. Hemet is mentioned right away. Wes doesn't come home for three days, and then he sleeps it off for two. It isn't that I love North Park any less than he does. I've grown to care quite a bit about the place, the little houses, the huge Balboa Park nearby. I've gotten to like the people.

One of Annie's sisters guesses that Willy has AIDS, and Annie comes undone. I tell her, "More people have AIDS these days. People know about it."

"They still don't accept it."

"At least they don't think you can get it off toilet seats anymore. You need your sister."

Archie starts stopping by to see Annie and Willy more often. They let him.

Wes asks, "When are we leaving?"

"Soon," I tell him. On top of everything else, Alice Matthews' Theatre hasn't given me any new leads, I'm tired of being a transmitter for people I don't know, and afraid I won't like Wes after another year.

Tiny and Ruby have us over for meat loaf. Ruby rips the inseam of her pink stretch pants bending over to bring out pictures of grandchildren. "What the hell, with his driving record off my policy, maybe my premiums will go down," Tiny says with tears in his eyes.

The last week, Cecil and some of the other jazz guys have Wes over. Later Wes tells me they lit fire to tequila and drank it in one shot, played short duets in the corner, as if to make it final, and then brought out a cake frosted to look like the Pacific Ocean.

On his way home, Wes stops for a beer with Chelsea and me at the Over Easy.

"Jazz isn't the same as classical," Wes implores when she's gone. "It doesn't have the long clear notes, the purity."

"We need a change."

"I don't know." He shakes his head.

I tell the phone company where to send my W-2 forms, give the Silver Springs water man back his dispenser, throw out Gantrisin from when I had a bladder infection in the summer of 2005, fill nail holes with toothpaste and pack.

"It's been two days," I tell Chelsea through the yellow receiver. "We're leaving Friday."

"In other words, you're doing all the work."

"I think he feels like a failure when he sees the boxes all over the house."

"Tell him to take a flying arabesque and come stay with me."

"Thanks anyway, Chelsea."

And then I pick up the phone again, put it down, pick it up and call.

"Hey, Towhead, it's the old lady," Cecil shouts across a room I know is full of blue snakes of smoke, tin music, coughing. "How ya been?"

"Busy moving."

"You can move old Towhead, but you can't change him. He's got it in his blood. Never heard quite the same coming from such a young trombone."

"It's not working out."

"Give the man some time, baby."

"Just tell old Towhead to blow or I'm jamming," I say and slap the phone down. I make my half of the bed for the third day in a row and leave Wes a note that I've gone to the Laundromat. At South Park Sudz, I wait until the clothes have spun dry, then carry them dripping to the industrial dryer. The rolling metal baskets are all being used by the same woman. She has generations of clothes to fold, varicose veins, a daughter crying in the corner. I don't want to listen so I read the bulletin board, which gives me phone numbers for tall singles, alternate lifestyles, drug hotlines, Samoan dance, and fingernail stylists. I take a copy of *Awake!* and sit on the corner outside.

Wes pushes through the glass door without speaking, begins throwing damp Levis, a shirt my mother and I found with trombones floating over the heart, and pillow slips into the large cardboard soap box.

"Why are you letting her cry like that?" I plead with the woman back inside.

"It's none of your business," the woman huffs. She turns and hangs a violet floral housedress.

"She's right, it isn't any of your business," Wes says.

"Wonderful." I throw damp curtains and bed pads into the box without folding and then Wes grabs the box.

On the street we silently race to keep up with each other.

"You shouldn't be talking to strangers at night anyway."

"Somebody has to say something."

On our driveway we pant while I fumble in my purse for the house keys and avoid each other's eyes. Wes throws the laundry on the floor.

"So why are you doing the laundry at this time of the night anyway?"

"It's only nine o'clock."

"This is a city neighborhood. It could be dangerous."

"No more dangerous than living in this house."

"What's that supposed to mean?"

"Living with you is about as comforting as living with a tire iron."

He slams me hard against the wall, right on my shoulder. I feel like something has broken.

"God, I'm sorry," Wes says, stunned. "How could I hurt you?" His hands cover eyes that have begun to water, then reach to help me. But I push him away.

"Leave me alone!" I say.

I run out to my car and drive the two hours to my parents' house. After she takes me to the doctor and I'm finished crying, I tell my mother, "Wes is just so full of ideas and feelings about things. He gets so frustrated about the music. It only happened once."

"A dislocated shoulder is something that should never happen at all," she says, finalizing her seed choices from the catalogs she's ordered, sliding them neatly into the corner of the cabinet.

When my father finds out, he drives all the way to Wes's office, confronts him on the street. Tells him if he ever lays a hand on his girl again, he'll have Wes locked up. The only girl, I've always been my dad's ballet dancer.

That Friday Wes and I move to Hemet.

Months go by and we simmer down, forget about the sharp

edges in the city. We hold hands even when we're only going to the Home Depot, a place neither of us wants to spend too much of our life.

It is a warm Hemet afternoon, and we're strolling down the canyon in what was once back country behind the trailer. Nimbus Cumulus lopes away and barks at stray cows and looks almost beautiful in the distance where one cannot see his funny proportions.

"I don't want any," I say when we have settled on a grassy plot and Wes hands me a joint. My words take time to register. The speeding cars on the new highway seem like they're in another dimension when I consider how long it took us to walk from a spot I can still see, when I compare the wind pushing nearby alfalfa weeds into gentle backbends.

"It can't be more than twenty yards across the road."

"When you think of all those people flying by in their cars."

At the top of the hill we look across the canyon, see the trailers perched there like mirrors at a hat counter. Red and white banners snap in the wind, try to attract the freeway's attention to the new shopping center.

I pause at the crest and see a dark shadow race down the hill. It is Nimbus Cumulus. I freeze, can only watch as he flies, tongue flapping at the side of his mouth, thinking those are like any other twenty yards. He steps tentatively onto the freeway. A car squirms and misses him. I sit down. Wes is watching too, but his long legs stretch down the hill.

"Don't!" I hear myself say.

He shouts something back, but he is years away, a whisper under swishing cars, semis.

Two cars screech. Nimbus Cumulus limps to the center divider and curls into a ball. Even though I'm far away, I know he's trembling.

Wes runs across the lanes, picks the dog up and then climbs the hill opposite me. I watch the strange couple, the skinny man with the huge animal in his arms. I watch the freeway, and then I walk home.

I don't see either of them when I return from the long way around the freeway. It is not hard to realize that our stay in Hemet will not last much longer. As easy as it is here, neither one of us is happy. I look forward to meeting up with Chelsea at Claire de Lune in North Park again, talking to Annie, watering the garden surrounding our cottage.

I hear whining on the side of the trailer. The crate has been turned over and Nimbus Cumulus is inside. Wes is shaking the crate, shouting for the trapped dog to come to him, scolding. I hear the dog bumping into the walls, scratching, and howling.

"Let him go, Wes."

"He might as well learn."

"Wes."

"He's boxed in like the rest of us."

"Let him go!"

Wes turns the crate over. He throws a sharp rock, splitting the dog's hind leg. Nimbus Cumulus has never shown his teeth like this before. He catches his bearings, slinks off to the park bathroom. Later I find the paw hit by the car is only slightly cut, but the rock has left a gash.

It is a long while before Nimbus Cumulus will allow Wes to come near him again. He cowers under the dinette, leaves puddles before darting out the door.

We go to Denny's, after a movie, discuss moving back.

"Nimbus'll be okay," Wes says, putting the tab on his Visa card. "He likes dog park."

"Yeah, maybe," I say, trying to see inside other people's cars on the ride home.

Back at the mobile home, I pick up the ringing phone. Chelsea's voice quivers at the other end. "I could just strangle myself," she says. "It's so typical. The old married man syndrome."

"How did it happen?" I sit down to listen.

"We bumped into his sister-in-law downtown. He said I was his receptionist and that he was taking me to lunch for my birthday. I said, 'My ass,' and left."

"What did *he* do?" I groan.

"Who the hell cares? Anyway . . . I met this disc jockey last weekend. He's only twenty-one, but so what?"

"Oh, Chelsea." I laugh into the phone. "You're nuts!"

"Like Alice Matthews says: One has to stay on one's toes."

Wes is offered a job at San Diego High School, School of the Arts.

"I'm not sure I'm ready to go back," I tell him.

"I can't stay here much longer," he says, pacing. "It doesn't start until January."

"Let's think about it."

When Nimbus Cumulus runs away, I check with Neophobia's owners. They haven't seen him. I take long walks in the woods. He isn't there. I leave out large bones with chunks of meat the size of silver dollars, chunks the coyote in him would have loved. He doesn't come back.

"You just can't explain these things," Wes is saying with my head in his lap, stroking the fine hairs by my temples, after driving me to the country, after I am dried of tears.

"But I didn't want him to leave. Why did it have to happen?"

"Maybe somebody stole him. You just can't tell." His voice is getting edgy.

I sit up. "You made him leave," I say. "If it wasn't for you, he wouldn't have left."

Wes moves away from me. "You can't keep a dog like that locked up in a trailer."

I stare. "If we go back, it will happen all over again."

He pulls my body close to his, so close I feel a little panicky. "It won't," he tells me. "I promise. If we stay here, I'll die."

I believe him, though I'm afraid. And I miss seeing the folks in the old neighborhood, that funny college girl, Heather, and whoever her current boyfriend is. The poor old guy, Edgar, who lived in North Park during the plane crash and who brightens up if you just say hello to him.

So I go through all the accumulations again, belongings that keep catching up with me: a poster of a rainbow my grandmother gave me for high school graduation, the key to my first apartment over a yogurt shop in Ocean Beach, leftover invitations to our wedding, a snapshot of my mother and me taken a year ago by the barbecue in her backyard. I see the same nose, identical jowls, a numbness about the eyes. I bury the picture in my suitcase, as far down as it will go, and pack.

Movement in the Wire

Out my window, I watch Cat Man tramp down the darkened sidewalk of our mostly-quiet neighborhood as he often does at 2:00 a.m., his bowl of livers in one hand, his bowl of kidneys in the other. "Kit! Kit! Kit! Kit!" he trills, only the moonlight guiding his way. Bloated and bent in his stockinged feet, he heads for the small traffic island and the orange glow cast by the street lamp. "Gotcha all covered, kits. Come to daddy."

Tonight, a Chevy fan belt abruptly shrieks like wild animals, out of control, on one side of the triangular island. Shivering in my nightgown, I'm home alone since John has gone to a group meeting at the hospital where he had to stay for three weeks last year.

I watch Cat Man duck by the palm tree and then shout, "Incoming!" An Impala bottoms out on the other side, rusted metal grinding asphalt. "Movement in the wire!" Cat Man cries, no doubt seeing Viet Cong creeping into home territory, an invasion. He flails to the ground, squirms his way over broken glass on his elbows, hides beside a parked car. He keeps a grip on the bowls, like they're C-rations, indispensable.

I turn my lights out. Transparent curtains in the murky adobe home across the way ripple abruptly, so I know Sabrina, the mother of the skateboarders, is vigilant, too. We know Cat Man has important front teeth missing. We know he sleeps all day. We know about the methadone. We watch his Craftsman bungalow deteriorate, his roof cave a little more every year, his porch sag. We cover for him, yet some nights when I make my way to the bodega for a bottle of wine, I cross the street so I don't have to pass his place alone. The other night I saw Annie at the corner store buying Jim Beam.

Two-story cathouses stacked like condos snuggle in by Cat Man's front door and often make me smile when I'm passing. Most folks don't like the ferals he keeps that multiply faithfully, but at least it's fun to watch the macaws swoop down to get cat hair for their nests.

One of the cathouse awnings says, "Cats only!" The other, "No dogs allowed!" Cats are always napping inside, on his dead Bermuda, his driveway, under Darts and Hyundais parked at the curb. Cats with missing eyes, smelly wounds, disease. Cats who won't let you near them, who scramble over fences, lurch from shrubs and alleys, stalk their pied piper, coveting their organs.

A slow car menaces. A window rolls down. Kids and heavy metal. Bass so omnipotent it hurtles into my place, rattles the walls.

"What the hell you doing under a car, ya stupid old man?" a boy's cracking voice shouts into damp air. The music cuts.

Crickets chirp their forewings, calling, mating, steadfast. There is laughter. Beer cans ping, chatter down the pavement. A pitched bottle soars, explodes, glass chinking against the glittery, moonlit sidewalk. Whoops, catcalls, dares. Car doors groan and boys wearing large Adidas jump out. My hand reaches for 911.

The old man runs for his life, flinging Styrofoam bowls skyward, livers and kidneys landing everywhere. Strays, lustful, arch suspiciously.

Cat Man's beer belly swings in his way. His legs move like they probably haven't since Southeast Asia, spinning, machines. He thuds headlong onto the dirt of his property, rolls under shrubs, into shadows, setting up a defense. Uncle Rempt, who must be home early from his oxygen business, stands barefoot in front of my place. Quiet. Watching. Baseball bat in hand. He knows I'm here.

The boys jump back in. Squealing tires charge after Cat Man. Burned rubber gasses the neighborhood. The car stalls in front of his place, and the driver thinks about it, the boys are ready, but then they move on. Felines scatter farther in the peeling wake, gravel spitting, voices knife-like, scary, high-pitched. They leap fences, sneak back to their alleys, others slithering through thistle and blue hibiscus, returning to the bungalow and its lighted porch. Cat Man slips furtively behind a palm, a jacaranda with lavender flowers. He finally makes it inside, screen banging.

Then cats converge on the sidewalk, dozens of them, wolfing.

Rempt jerks his head toward my window. I nod. We scan the bushes, the darkness, the block.

No more VC.

A Black Sea

Alexa spun, finally fed up with the manufacturing talk at the Hotel Delfin in Playas De Rosarito, Baja, Mexico. She abruptly removed herself from the droning group of men downing cocktails in the lobby reception. Men, that is, and one horrid female exec from El Paso who kept hanging on Eduardo. I've been good, Alexa told herself. I've kept my mouth shut about their funny business. She'd only agreed to come to his conference because he'd promised to take her to Guadalupe Valley to see the haciendas and wineries. She didn't have to watch this woman throwing herself on her man, even if Eduardo did have to humor her for business purposes.

The ride down across the border from San Diego had been hot as Hades, as though they'd brought the Santa Ana winds to Baja with them. The air conditioning in the old Mustang didn't work, making the ten-mile ride from Tijuana to Rosarito even worse. Dense chaparral, jojoba, and yucca subsisting on almost no water possessed the hills left of the toll road while the ocean slammed onto shore to the west. One hundred degree winds charged them at eighty miles an hour, kicking up dust and sand, causing rivulets of sweat to run down Alexa's body, heating her to the brink.

Together five years, she and Eduardo had been married only one, and Alexa wanted more attention. "Have I lost you?" she sometimes said, batting her eyelashes and trying to make a joke of it when she was getting ready to paint and he was leaving for work in the morning. A paintbrush full of red or yellow in her hand, she threatened to color him.

"I'm sorry, baby," he said, kissing her at the door. "*Te quiero, mi reina.*"

"You two are weird together, I admit," Lenora from down the street had said just yesterday sitting on Alexa's patio. "The artiste and the executive, but you share a certain fire."

"I just wish he didn't work so much," Alexa said.

"You have a right to ask him to spend more time with you."

That's when Heather and her UPS man had a spat. The strange dynamic of the apartment balcony above all the one-story bungalows was that their voices ricocheted through everyone's driveways and backyards, making whatever they were saying undeniably clear.

"Stop asking me what you should major in, dude," the UPS guy told Heather.

"Why won't you help me?"

"I can't make all your decisions for you."

Sean the surf boy had been seen in the neigborhood again. Not that he'd moved home. He made it clear he'd never do that again. Sabrina and Neil were just glad he was okay. Sean and Susan, who'd moved from Aloha with her Uncle Rempt, were now said to be quite the young couple, apparently living near the beach in some back room they rented by the month. Word was she breathed a lot of oxygen and he surfed. Her strange uncle visited frequently and made sure they were okay, though who decided he'd be good for the job was beyond her.

The truth was Alexa loved the morning light and most everything else about their part of town. The brilliant-colored succulents inspired her work, the occasional macaws. At least her husband was hearty and not wasting away like Annie's husband Willy next door. At least Eduardo lived with her, unlike the lady friend of Ramón Fernández, the sweet older gentleman who lived around the corner. His woman, Lucinda—bubbly and kind—was afraid of moving in with him and losing her independence.

But Alexa did struggle with a vast emptiness inside and longed for what had gone missing in her marriage. She also missed herself.

At the Hotel Delfin, Alexa stepped onto the ballroom floor and stalked across the terra cotta tiles to get away from her husband's business group. Her rich black hair splayed out behind her, and she could feel rills of cool droplets cascading down the heat of her back. Eduardo and his business buddies, as well she knew, weren't staring only at her hair but at her ass as well. She wagged it a little extra. She deserved to have some fun.

"Alexa!" Eduardo called after her, so that now all the business types were staring, including that broad from El Paso. He winked, but Alexa knew he was probably pissed that she was acting up. She didn't need it. If he wasn't going to keep his promise about the drive, she'd engross herself in the folk art exhibit in the far corner of the room. She wanted to see the Day of the Dead paper-mache creatures and the Guatemalan Santos the hotel had advertised besides the hand-carved Oaxacan *alebrijes* Eduardo's company planned to mass-produce out of pressed sawdust. Authentic *alebrijes*, or monsters, often carved from a single piece of wood, emerged as whimsical bats, dogs, and goats painted in psychedelic yellow, orange, and green. Sometimes the shapes were unidentifiable since they came from the subconscious of the artisan. These beasts carried the notion that every human has a spiritual animal counterpart.

"Another cabernet, Señora Ramírez?" asked a waiter as she marched past. Hair fluttering over her neck and back coupled with the muscular curves of her body, she'd been told, made her look pleasingly equine.

"No, thank you," she said, and smiled, grateful to keep her temper in check for at least this small exchange.

Eduardo had been an architecture major. It wasn't his fault he couldn't get a job in the field he was most ardent about and so had taken this one. Still. She was being too hard on him, she knew.

But besides just missing him, there was something between them that had changed.

She peeked back. The blond business lady from El Paso now leaned so closely into Eduardo her breasts nudged him, and she was picking nits off his lapels—the cunning monkey. The cunning monkey had been the one to say, "Let's face it, if the Oaxacans had had factories for the last few decades, they'd have manufactured the little gewgaws themselves."

Gewgaws? The woman was disgusting. Alexa took off farther across the ballroom until suddenly Eduardo grabbed her arm and swung her around to face him. "What are you doing? Are you trying to ruin this? C'mon, I just got the job. Let's try to get along."

"Don't you touch me!" she said, but the truth was mostly she wished he'd touch her more. They'd hardly made love lately, not since he'd begun working endless hours, came home exhausted. But when they did, she floated for days. His gentle roughness magnified her own urges. He gazed on her single-mindedly, as if she didn't exist but for the sexual creature she was, bewitching, able to satisfy what burned. She felt gratification in being only sexual sometimes, in letting go of everything else.

"First, I'm supposed to call all the wives," she said, tapping her foot impatiently on the ballroom floor.

"I know it's not your thing." Eduardo smiled apologetically. "But somebody had to call them. Management wanted the wives to feel welcome at the conference."

"But why me? They're not paying me anything."

"Because we're new."

She leaned on her hip, angled her face up in his direction. "So I'm automatically part of the firm, too? What about me and who I am?"

Other women noticed Eduardo. His hefty mustache brooded over an ample mouth and cleft chin, and his full eyebrows, like nests, made his gaze unforgettable. He was slightly overweight, but his carriage made him seem stately and grand. He looked better than most in his *guayabera*, a Mexican wedding shirt with embroidery down the front worn casually even in San Diego. His terracotta-colored skin contrasted nicely with the muslin. His huskiness, warmth, and towering stature reminded her of a bear.

"And why did I have to be the one to give a talk on Rosarito Beach at their meeting?" she said. "I love Rosarito, but do they understand I'm Greek, Eduardo? Have you ever mentioned I'm not Mexican, or do they think everyone with black hair is?"

"I told you, Alexa. They wanted you to feel like you were a part of the group."

She whispered loudly, "No matter what that horrid woman says, families make their livings off the *alebrijes!*"

He laughed and reached for her again, saying, "The little monsters only cost a few bucks on the street. That tells you how important they are."

Moving away, like they were dancing a complicated salsa, back and forth, she said, "They represent what goes on inside us. You have to believe in some things you can't see, Eduardo. That's what makes them beautiful."

"Alexa."

"You should have married someone more agreeable."

"You were always the one, Alexa. You know that. You bring out the life in me." The glint in his eyes confused her, as if he was laughing at her, yet she knew he meant it.

The sun faded outside the ballroom, and the execs from Eduardo's firm watched them intently, as did bellboys, food handlers, the conference director, and attendees. Waitpersons gliding across the tiles with trays of pork carnitas and chiles rellenos adjusted their paths to avoid the tempestuous couple. A security guard took a few steps closer just in case. The overhead fan caused the only movement of air in the whole room. Alexa's clothes stuck to her skin.

"Don't you like our house?" Eduardo said, fists jammed into his waist, pushing his suit jacket behind him and making his shoulders mountainous. "Or food? I have to do business."

"I know." It was true. He'd graciously supported her during the four years since they'd graduated. He didn't complain. He hadn't played soccer, one of his passions, in over a year.

Why did she have to be such a monster?

"You think we can live on your salary?" he asked.

She taught part time, making a pittance, at workshops in the local schools. She liked to think she taught kids to dream.

"Let's give up the house, *mi amor*," she said, finally moving closer. "We'll sell it and stop worrying about money. You can throw yourself into your designs. I miss you, Eduardo."

A gruff laugh while they embraced. Sometimes, like now, she felt that all was not lost. They still hugged. They still cared. But there was an edge.

"Or you could get a better job and take some of the pressure off me."

Though there was something true about this, she threw his arms from her body. She didn't want a more serious job.

"Come here," he said, pulling her back.

"I miss how we used to go camping and sleep under the stars," she said.

Glancing over at his partners, his voice softened. "Do you want to fight about everything?" Removing a handkerchief from his pocket, he dabbed his forehead and neck.

"Yes!"

"Why?" he said, smirking.

"Because of how you want me so much afterward."

"How can I get you to behave?" he grumbled. He hugged her, kissed her neck. "You better be ready for what I'm going to do to you in about a half an hour. That dress is a disgrace." His eyes bore through the gauze bodice of what she was wearing, only mildly see-through, perfectly acceptable, except where Eduardo was concerned

Heat rose from her body.

His hands jammed into his pockets, adjusting. "That's a big help," he said.

"You promised me the drive."

"It's already late afternoon."

"I'm feeling wild," Alexa said, "locked up. I need to get outside and smell the ocean."

His eyes glowed at her, but just then the cunning monkey waved over at him, showing a lot of teeth as she laughed, a gash of garish lipstick, waving her pinky finger as if Alexa wasn't even there. Eduardo smiled at her.

Alexa charged into the women's room, Eduardo in close pursuit.

"Alexa! This isn't funny." He lit a smoke. "That woman means nothing to me."

At the sound of his voice, women popped out of stalls like cuckoo clocks, ran quickly from the room.

"If we don't leave soon," she said, "I'll hitchhike back up to Tijuana."

Minutes later, they pushed through the lobby's large Spanish doors. At the entry to the hotel, they passed a fountain of Neptune shooting water from his penis.

Alexa threw herself onto the ragged but soft corduroy seat of Eduardo's ancient Mustang convertible. He'd had it forever but was in the process of deciding what new car he'd buy now that he had a job that paid decently

"Let's take the free road, okay?" she said. "So we can see some of the different villages?" She turned in her seat to watch the last rays of the sun lingering over a black sea.

"If you weren't so insecure," Eduardo said, exiting the lot, "I could make more deals." He squinted, struggling to pay attention as they took off. There were no guard rails and no highway lamps as they headed into a more rural Baja.

"Don't you understand? This has nothing to do with that woman. Don't blame this on me!"

"Shut up," he said. "Just shut up. This whole business sucks me dry."

"Yeah, and none of you is left for me."

They drove in silence, made headway down the free road. Only backcountry surrounded them now. Moonlike, not a car in sight, it felt like a place few humans had ever seen, this world made of golden grasses, sand dunes, occasional blue-green palm trees, as well as dusty cactus and chaparral. Foreboding cliffs shot past the windows on the right, rough mountains to the left. Sunlight waned, shadows elongated, though the heat continued to be insufferable.

"You don't even know me."

"What are you talking about?" He shifted gears fiercely, squealed around corners.

"Sometimes I hate you..."

"You only hate me so you can love me more when the time comes."

Road signs for Ensenada ticked by. What she wanted was for Eduardo to feel what she felt when she was alone with a canvas in their garage, boxes piled up in the corners, old sleeping bags, golf clubs. She needed to be able to see without interference from the world, to see inside herself, to see what mattered. Eduardo used to need this, too. When she was painting murals, the colors knowing where they went without her needing to intervene, she was most alive, regardless of how dark and obscure others might see her work. She wanted Eduardo to feel this magic again, like he used to with architecture, like they'd been able to share in college. They used to buy groceries for the weekend at the corner bodega, hole up in their old apartment, hardly dress or speak the entire weekend— though they did make love. She longed for how he used to be the one person she could count on, who shared her belief that life was bigger than all the daily nonsense, that it was about all the possibilities generated by the human mind. That part of him seemed to be disappearing, no longer available to her.

"What'll we be like in five years if we already don't connect?" she asked.

"Stop it."

"I can't."

He pounded his hand on the steering wheel, his wedding ring snapping against the plastic. "We aren't kids anymore. It's time to grow up."

"What's that supposed to mean?"

"People have to have jobs to live. You should be proud of me."

Alexa shook her head. "But that doesn't mean we have to give all our other beliefs up."

"Hell!" Eduardo plowed off the free road, as if proving he wasn't all about the straight and narrow, drove several miles inland on a rutted country one, dirt, manipulating the car back and around doglegs up a hill.

"What are you doing?" Alexa said.

He steered them off even the side road, as if he could get away from the argument altogether, stopping abruptly in a dirt gully, the tires hitting loose soil, whirring, not going anywhere. Dirt spewed, rocketed behind them. Silt mushrooms settled onto the windows, making the whole area a dusty wonderland. The afternoon had grown darker.

"Shit!" Eduardo said.

He threw the car door open and heaved himself out. "I can't drive when you get like this. I've got to walk around a minute."

"Fine." Opening the passenger door, she was immediately besieged by clay dust. The earth felt unstable under her feet, like right after an earthquake when it wasn't clear whether things were still moving or not.

Eduardo, obscured by the vast particles of dust ambushing the air, appeared to glare all around them. Visibility was made worse by the headlights reflecting against the swirling grit. The Santa Ana winds whooshed through, branches bowing into unnatural poses.

"Is this what you meant by fresh air?" he said. He kicked at some rocks, then set off wandering up a path on the side of the bluff. Alexa stayed out of his way. At her side, a large cactus with a multitude of needles seemed to stick its tongue out; a tall stock with pendulous orange petals spit right out its middle. Cream-colored lilies, knee high, scattered about underfoot. The Mustang's headlights shot uphill and prevented the bluff from being entirely swallowed by the darkening shadows. Eduardo and Alexa crept past dried vegetation. Spiky trees bent, trying to reach them. Beans growing on a woody shrub scraped their ankles.

To their right, that's where they saw it—an abandoned campfire. Surrounded by brambles, an animal appeared to be lying just outside the fire ring, though the dust was still swirling through the car lights.

"There's something wet over there by it," Alexa said.

"Where?"

"Is it blood?"

"Don't touch anything."

Maybe the moonlight was hitting the dirt in a strange way, an odd shadow. They crept off the path to look closer.

A dead dog. Mutilated.

"What the hell's going on here?" Eduardo said.

Alexa seemed unable to talk, then heard herself say, "A coyote? Hunters?"

But they both knew that wasn't it, not with the long nail marks raked over the dog's corpse.

Turning immediately back for the car, Eduardo couldn't stop staring. "What killed it?

"Maybe someone or something couldn't hold it all in anymore and went on a spree."

"Hold what in? What are you talking about?"

Alexa paused, eyeing what still looked like blood. Or was it animal tracks illuminated in the shadows? Something trying to slip away and get back to its origins? She thought about the boy, Sean, mysteriously disappearing for a while, seeming like he was he was never going to return from the beach, his parents brokenhearted. Is that what would happen with her and Eduardo, they'd just disappear from this backcountry, only unlike Sean, nobody would ever hear from them again?

She and Eduardo watched closely as if the scene would suddenly become clear. They could not seem to leave. Besides, whatever had happened was already over.

Alexa started walking upward, toward the summit of the hill.

"What are you doing?" Eduardo said. "We have to get out of here." He turned to hike the other way, back down to the bottom.

"I have to find out what's going on," she said.

"This is dangerous, *reina*," Eduardo told her, concerned. "We don't need to be the ones. Someone else, the *policía*, will come along during daylight." He stood closer to her than he had since the beginning of their spat.

"But how can we ignore it?"

A crunchy sound that could have been footsteps unleashed itself, and the two of them stiffened, not saying another word until several minutes had passed.

"Are you okay?" Eduardo finally said, his voice breaking. He reached for her hand, which she happily gave him.

"I don't know."

They backed up, turned, faced the crest of the bluff.

"All I can see besides stars," Eduardo said, "is that shed up top. We have to be careful."

"I'm so tired of being careful," Alexa murmured. Like Eduardo, though, she stopped any movement. She tried to focus better, to make her senses more acute, to feel what was happening. But dust continued throwing itself at them, blown in by the cutting desert winds, howling through the valley. Turbulent dry gales rustled through bushes, swooshed her hair, swept sand into her nose and eyes.

Eduardo hugged her. "Something's wrong here. This isn't safe, and I don't want anything to happen to you."

She leaned into his hug.

Gazing toward the heavens, he stepped away towards the path again and to the road leading up the hill. "Wait here. I'm going to see if it's safe to go back to the car."

He climbed several hundred yards before noticing she was right behind him.

"Alexa," he said, halting and facing her. "Stop."

But she held her ground. "I can't just stand around and wait."

The moon and car beams illuminated their bleak surroundings, but still didn't make anything clear, not with the wind. She and Eduardo stared up the hill, leaning against each other. She could detect the outline of the abandoned building he had pointed towards, but not much more—perhaps a barn, worn from sea gusts. After exploring their surroundings and climbing the hill, her elegant dress had developed small tears in the coral gauze, and one of her spaghetti straps had broken. Twigs in her long hair, jostled by the breeze, scratched her shoulders. Eduardo pierced his finger on a cactus needle. He smelled sweaty, and his Mexican wedding shirt now had sand stuck in the white embroidery. His arms dwarfed her, his hands rested at her small waist. Alexa burrowed her head in his chest. He put his bloody finger in his mouth.

"What's that?" he said suddenly.

She stood straight again.

Something was there, something big and muscular if her eyes weren't tricking her. A foul smell overtook the bluff, so strong even the wind couldn't dilute it—tangy, excremental, like deteriorating flesh. She tried to focus her eyes. What looked like teeth reflected back. Or could moonlight simply be pinpointing a portion of the brilliant white sandstone? The teeth slavered like a pit bull's. The jaws ratcheted like a shark's. It appeared to be loping towards them.

A face. For a second she thought she saw a face, reptilian, half human.

"*Qué chingados?*" Eduardo shouted.

Alexa screamed and galloped toward the car, Eduardo right behind her, their progress impeded only when they nearly tripped over an obstacle heaped in the dirt. Her eyes bore down trying to fathom what it was, and when she understood, she screamed again. Her shoes touched a dead burro, another dead dog, both mutilated. The grotesque being didn't seem to have followed, but just because they couldn't see him didn't mean he wasn't there. Blood seeped from the neck of each of the dead beasts. The skin around the wounds was ashen. They'd been exsanguinated.

"Their blood was sucked!" she shouted at Eduardo.

"What?"

"Look at their necks!"

Knowing they had to get away, but unsure of what direction to go, she backed up while Eduardo stared. The odor of the carcasses—or was it the thing itself?—permeated the area, sickeningly sweet, fetid, rancid. That's when they heard a raw, piercing screech. She and Eduardo reached for each other, and though she wanted to run, Eduardo whispered, "Slow. We don't want it to see us," as they inched down the hill.

"What in god's name is it?" she said.

Just then something jumped twenty feet in the air, clearing the rickety old shed at the top. How could it have moved so fast when it had just been standing not too far away? The silhouette they saw, thought they saw, through the dust and the dim light, depicted the being springing over the out building with tremendous agility despite seeming heavy, as if there were seven feet of it in the blurry moonlight. An owl with an incredibly large wing span? Were those wing beats she heard? A kangaroo? Enormous thighs seemed to be doing the hurdling. She and Eduardo shrieked. Grabbing hands, they fled the rest of the way down the hill. The sound of the car keys jingling in Eduardo's hand had never been more reassuring.

"Hurry!" Eduardo said. But she didn't have to be encouraged. "You sit and steer," he told her when they reached the car. "I'll push."

She took off the emergency break, and immediately they rolled out of the soft dirt, Eduardo forcing his weight against the trunk.

"Switch with me. Quick!" he said.

They passed each other running around the hood of the car. Eduardo started the engine before she'd even closed her door.

She kept quiet as he blasted the car further out of the earth, the engine whining, the gears shifting, the Mustang finally lurching ahead, out of the gully, down the doglegs. Gravel shot out behind them like ammunition as they spun out on the worn asphalt of the free road. Soon they were speeding, craning their necks frequently to make sure the thing wasn't following.

"Is it there, honey?" Eduardo said. "Do you see anything?" He studied the rearview mirror at least as much as he did the road ahead of them.

"I can't see anything. I don't know." Drained of everything that had been so lively inside of her not so long ago, she twisted her body and neck into an uncomfortable position and stayed that way to study the skies out the back window, on guard for anything that shouldn't be there. The fact that it was dark made no difference. She could not *not* look. And with such an amorphous creature, who knew what she would see anyway.

"Can you drive faster?" she asked Eduardo, without turning around.

"These damn curves! You see anything? I need to know. Anything?"

Alexa shook her head.

He asked her again two minutes later and ninety seconds after that.

She was afraid to move, afraid that if she relaxed even a second, the creature now lying in wait would attack.

They flew through La Fonda, Punta Mesquite, got onto the toll road and then onto Benito Juarez Boulevard in town.

"What was it?" he finally said, his shoulders still pinched up to his ears.

"Something awful and ugly," she said.

"That was sheer sadism, the way it killed those animals. Hurting for the sake of hurting."

"I think it needed the blood." Alexa scratched her stinging eyes. "But I hope to god we never see it again." She turned and looked back.

"Do you think we're going to make it?" he said. "Do you think it can catch up with us?"

Alexa rubbed her arms at the thought, though the Santa Ana was still every bit as oppressive at this time of night. The clock on the dashboard read 9:00 p.m.

She could see he was still as frightened as she was—the glances out the rearview, the way he still hadn't leaned back in his seat. She flushed with sympathy for him. She should never have complained about her life. She didn't need trouble. Her neighbor Lenora was right. She didn't have to be angry to ask for more time with her husband. Why couldn't she be more like Lenora? Though it would be hard to have a husband like John, flying high part of the time, barely able to pick himself off the floor the other. Just because words failed her, though, didn't mean it didn't hurt that lately it had been hard to find the love she used to feel for Eduardo.

"You sure you still don't see anything?" he said, speeding with no concern for the *federales*. "Scoot over next to me, baby. We're going to be fine."

She moved as close as she could to his warmth, but wished she felt more convinced that the monster was gone forever.

"That thing could catch up with us," she said, feeling stuck inside her body. "Couldn't we get off the road so we're not out in the open? We could pull into one of these little motels."

He considered the row of darkened beach shacks. "That thing had weird powers."

Within minutes, he'd parked in front of a sign that said Casa del Agua, close to the water, but not in high demand judging by the deserted appearance. They sprang from the car and hurried to the motel's office door. Eduardo rang the buzzer three times. Waves pounded on the sand nearby, the vibrations shaking the ground beneath them.

"*Cuál es el problema?*" the awakened manager said when he finally opened the door. "What's the noise?"

"Can we come in?" Alexa asked.

The manager waved his hand wearily through the entryway, but once he'd shut the door, he studied their faces.

"*Qué paso?*" he said.

"You wouldn't believe us."

The manager's jeans slung low over his hips, probably just thrown on, his hips protruding like a wishbone. "*Sí?*" He sat on a plastic beach chair. The corners of the walls were mildewed from the sea air.

"There's something huge out there," Alexa started. "It smelled bad and there was blood."

"We think it was chasing us," Eduardo said, as they gauged the man's reaction.

The manager sat up straight. "Like a kangaroo?"

"Or a lizard," Alexa said.

"The body was like a dog's," Eduardo said.

The manager rose from the chair, unsettled. "Goat sucker." He moved to the door and locked it. "A *chupacabra*." He pushed the shade on a window so he could peer out. "They live in the hills and leave goats and other animals in their paths. They suck the organs of the animals through very small openings. Especially the heart. They like the heart. They take most of the blood, too."

Alexa leaned against the wall. Sand had been tracked everywhere in the office.

"Are they real?" she asked the manager. "You've heard of them before?"

"*Ay*," he said, nodding. "Not everybody believes. But we have them in town. They steal our chickens."

"Where did they come from?"

"First Puerto Rico, then Mexico and the southwestern states."

"I need to get my wife to a room," Eduardo said. "We've been through hell."

"*Sí*." The manager seemed to understand immediately. He grabbed his keys off a nail, peered out the window again, then pulled the door open, inspecting both sides of the stoop. They followed him as he hurried across a courtyard and into a small, not unclean room. They gave no date as to when they would cross back over the border. Without speaking, Alexa bolted the entry, and Eduardo pushed a chair and then a dresser against it. They checked and double checked that the windows were locked, then sat, their backs leaning on the door, sweating.

Later, on the bed, Eduardo finally fell into a light sleep, but Alexa could not. It was terror, but also the guilt of realizing how mesmerized she was with the *chupacabra*, even attracted to it—the passion, the way it ripped what it needed from life and moved on. She imagined jumping beside one, becoming airborne with it, liberated. The creature craved something seemingly impossible to satisfy.

Eduardo woke to Alexa's distress and rubbed her back. "Can you let it go, *reina*, so you can sleep?" he said. "I don't think we'll ever see anything like that again."

"Really?"

"I swear."

"I'm not sure that's a good thing."

"*Alexa*." He pulled her head to his chest, grabbed a handful of her hair, kneading it through his fingers.

"Sometimes I feel like I'm disappearing," she said. "Sometimes I think it's good to hurt so much so I know I'm still alive, so I know something matters."

"I love you, Alexa. Nothing's going to happen. We're together."

"I'm going to get a better job, Eduardo."

"No, I love what you do, baby. Look, I'll quit my job if you don't care about being poor for a while. I want us both to be happy."

She kissed his neck, his nose, bit at his ear.

Eventually, nestled far underneath the covers, listening to the lapping waves, they held each other, slept on and off, fitfully in the heat. In the middle of the night, Alexa finally let go and wept uncontrollably. Eduardo awoke and stroked her. She moved her face back and forth against his tough whiskers, comforting herself. Soon they were torso to torso. Guttural noises vented from their room as they made love for hours, scratches swelling on each other's skin from holding each other so tight, their blood leaving its mark on the sheets.

Rocks

Everything is red. Giant rock formations inflame the town, russet pebbles live naturally by the side of the road, maroon homes made of adobe seem carved out of the pinnacles instead of built new. The rust is ore, the mark of a small ocean from millions of years ago, the formations from ancient earthquakes. Lolly is drawn to and repelled by the passionate siennas, the rosy salmons, the oppressive pink-grays, the turbulent bronze. Red has bled into the earth, color boundaries ignored, out of control.

What if Roy finds her?

"Ready for your maiden voyage, Lolly?" the manager whispers.

They're in the tour bus office in downtown Sedona. Visitors perch on wood benches bolted to a cement floor, waiting for the next departure. Lolly perches with them. Blond with tennis shoes and shorts and not so many years from graduating high school, she's new and antsy, and they have no idea that she will be their tour guide, the one driving.

"Of course," Lolly says. "Just a sec."

She rushes to the bathroom and spits up into the toilet again. She's spoken in front of people before, so why is she nauseated? Maybe because she lied to get the job. While no expert on Sedona, Arizona, she's long loved the town, visited on family trips when she was a girl, studied it from San Diego, California. Her real name isn't Lolly either.

She misses her old apartment in North Park, the plants zealous and blooming in the warm air, the boys' school only a few blocks over, the friendly next-door neighbor, Lenora, who teaches continuing ed. Lenora's husband John seemed nice enough as well, though for a while there he was taking a bus every day and seemed to be missing a lot of work. But Lolly could never really get to know the neighbors as much as she'd have liked, no matter how kind Lenora was or how concerned. She seemed to know something was wrong. Getting to know Lenora would have meant explaining to her about Roy, and Roy has made it clear that if she tells anybody about what's going on, including the police, he'll kill not only her but her parents.

"All aboard," she says loud as she can and climbs the steps onto the bus.

"Time to get on, sweetheart?" a man with binoculars and two cameras demands, seeming not to have heard her. Too authoritative to even sit, he's been hovering at the bus door since he arrived, leather straps crisscrossing his shirt. Even though she's sponged as many facts as she can on other tours, Lolly can tell this man will ask too many questions, questions she won't know the answers to.

Leaning over the enormous steering wheel, she uses shoulder muscle to crank the vehicle onto Highway 89. A red-tailed hawk glides overhead. The town teems with sightseers and tacky baubles—fake saguaro, tomahawks, overpriced tees. Four vortexes reside here, though, more than anywhere else in the world. Healing, soothing vortexes. Lolly needs them in the worst way.

"To our left," she says into the mike, the rattling chassis competing with her voice, "that's a butte—the tall, narrow hill, flat on top. Over there, that's a mesa—it has a flat top, too, but it's wider and lower." Rocks teeter from the sides of the road. They'd be on the asphalt, too, if humans didn't constantly prod them back.

She is one step ahead. Her boys, Brad and Thomas, are five and seven and safely in school in Cottonwood, the next town over. She's put five hundred miles between herself and Roy now, which should be plenty, except for Roy being Roy.

The binocular man bends at the knee, peers out the windshield over her shoulder, adobe architecture fleeing past on the right and the left. "So tell me, young lady, how do people afford to live here?"

"I'll get to that soon." She hopes he hasn't figured out she's a beginner. She needs to draw a line to protect herself from him, something she's no good at.

"In 1950, the first telephone arrived in Sedona," she announces on the microphone. "A public rest room followed in 1980." She watches in the rearview as tourists grin. "There," she points, "if you look carefully you'll see the Snoopy formation, nose and feet up, like he's lying on top of his doghouse, Woodstock on his belly." The allusion seems disrespectful of the area's spirituality, but it's part of the spiel.

She lets the group out to photograph Teapot Rock while she explains the century plant, an agave that blooms yellow flowers with sharp tips. Hummingbirds nest in the pod, thorns deterring predators, hurting those who get too close to their chicks. All she keeps seeing, though, is that red spot on the Navajo white wall back home in North Park, the one against which Roy heaved their oldest this time, the boy's soft forehead making a terrible cracking sound on the hard surface. She cannot allow that to happen again. The last time, when she simply ran to her parents', Roy came over and threatened to hurt them, so she had to go more miles this time. When no one's looking, she slips behind a manzanita and vomits.

The tourists feed themselves back onto the bus in an orderly manner, and soon they're bouncing against dusty ruts again while she mimics the old-timer tour guides, "We like to say that God may have created the Grand Canyon, but He lives in Sedona."

She sticks her elbow out the window, drives with one hand. She could get used to this tour guide thing—driving around, showing people the beauty of the desert.

She pulls over a second time. "Over to the right you can see a formation of Madonna and child." She's awestruck every time she sees the vivid limestone mother protecting her baby from the elements. Howling winds and ancient oceans have gnawed away at the rock to create her.

Trees and cactus grow straight out of rocks in Sedona. If that's the only way they can survive, that's what they'll do.

On the road, they pass a residential area, so now Lolly offers, "The land is expensive, but the cost of living isn't." In truth, she doesn't know how anybody can afford to live here, but she's happy with the trailer she's rented in Cottonwood. The boys like it there. The people are friendly.

"The cost of living's got to be steep, honey," the binocular man says, never far away. Fortunately, it's time to turn the corner back into town, and she ignores him.

She's almost succeeded on her first trip. That's when she sees him. It's definitely Roy: the handlebar moustache, the tattoo on his neck, the army boots. Her hands immediately go clammy, the muscle over her eye twitches and distorts, her heart pummels her chest wall so brutally she knows it's going to break.

She's supposed to pull up right in front of the office, but she drives by instead. If she stops, her life will stop, too. At least she has control of the wheel. But her mind flashes warnings—if he's here, he knows Brad and Thomas are here, too. She has to do something.

"Hey, sweetheart," the binocular man says immediately, "we just passed the office."

Quickly, she steers the rumbling bus onto a red curb, the voices onboard growing louder, more excited. She's engaged the brakes so abruptly that one of the passengers' overhead packages crashes to the floor, and a woman screams. Lolly releases the lever to the door and escapes.

Racing between boisterous tourists carrying parcels, she flees to the next block, turns onto a dark patio and sits behind a yucca tree, breathing hard. She will never leave this spot. Another red-tailed hawk seems to have followed her, circling above. Is it the same one as earlier?

Though she's hidden behind a yucca branch, she can still see. It's not Roy. It's another man carrying himself with a commanding gait like Roy's, a man who's slight but determined like Roy. One look at his laugh lines, though, the friendly arrangement of his mouth, and it's obviously not him.

She inhales so deeply her body inflates.

The man continues on into the brilliant red distance while the raptor soars above her, slow measured wing beats, circling constantly.

Lucinda's Song

The night Ramón Fernández first turned up at Sunday bingo hosted by the Sisters of the Precious Blood, Lucinda Sánchez couldn't have cared less. He and all those old hussies in attendance could kiss her eighty-year-old ass. And, frankly, it wasn't such a bad ass. They might be surprised.

Lucinda had been playing bingo at Mission San Luis Rey north of San Diego every Sunday evening for years. What did she care if a new person came, male or female? But three-quarters of the ladies playing that night—those old *viejas*—seemed to care and hot-footed it over to Ramón's table that first night they saw him, causing a racket as they battled for nearby seats. They offered up lucky ladybugs to help his chances, charmed gerbils, trolls, rabbits' feet and miniature Buddhas (kept hidden from the Sisters, naturally). They even turned lucky photos of their grandchildren in his direction. The old broads offered Ramón wily female instinct when it came to keeping his cards straight, like it was a mystery he'd made it to age seventy-eight without their help.

Fine with Lucinda. More breathing space at her end of the hall. She did catch him peering her way more than once, a warm smile, kindly eyes, a raised brow of crazy white hairs curling off in wayward directions despite the hair on his head being the deepest black color. She'd always been attracted to Indian men. Not that she was attracted. Only occasionally did she wonder about the opposite sex anymore. She rarely got lonely, and there was always her son, Miguel, across town.

"*Madre!*" he said when he'd called a few days ago. "The homeowner's association called me again. They say your flowers are dying."

"It's none of their business. They're my dead flowers, *mijo.*"

"They say they've sent you letters. You don't want to get kicked out."

"I don't have time for their damn letters. I'm an old woman. Why I have to live in this damn gated community is beyond me. I'd just as soon have stayed in my old place in North Park where all my old friends are."

"Because it's safer, Mama. I want you to be safe. There's an association to look after you if anything seems wrong."

"I can take care of myself."

"When Dad died, you said you'd try this. You didn't want to stay in that old house anyway, not after all those years dealing with him."

Her spot directly below the cross of Jesus Christ Our Savior in the bingo hall was what made her feel safe. Jesus had looked after her during those horrible years with her husband, Emilio. He'd protected her and Miguel from things getting worse, and He protected her still. Not only did Lucinda not have the slightest interest in repeating her history with men, she didn't have the energy. This Ramón Fernández might have kindly eyes, but she had no doubt he'd hook right up with one of the peppier sixty-three-year-old gals.

When she glanced back at Ramón in the bingo hall, he was looking her way again.

She propped a picture of her grandson, Oscar, in its luckiest position—on the very perimeter of her twenty bingo cards, each taped safely to the table. Then she aligned the photo under the cross on the wall, systematically arranging her daubers, which were filled with glittery ink to mark her cards with different colors. Her son was in the picture, too, which was unfortunate since he seemed to be glaring at her.

"So what's your big problem?" she asked Miguel's image softly. "Your mother gets out of the house and loses a little money? Like it's a sin?" She draped a piece of Kleenex, the one she kept shoved up the sleeve of her sweater, over Miguel's side of the picture so only the sweet eyes of her little grandson glimpsed out at her for luck. She lifted the Kleenex for one last second to tell her son, "Don't worry so much, *mijo*."

She'd been raised in the tradition that women must listen to what the males said, even their own sons. But she was tired of that old nonsense.

At this point in the summer, Lucinda Sánchez's lawn was still a beautiful shade of green. One of the biggest bothers about the subdivision was that she was supposed to keep all the plants "vibrant." Why that son of hers had picked this particular sterile community was beyond her. She sprinkled enough water to keep the association happy, though she'd just as soon have done away with the lawn altogether and planted a drought-tolerant ground cover. So a few flowers died when she wasn't looking. So what?

"You think you should be driving at night anymore, *Madre*?" Miguel asked when he called after her bingo game, the night she first saw Ramón. "I worry about you." Lucinda could hear clattering in the background, his wife doing the dishes.

"When I decide I can't drive anymore, I'll let you know. Don't put me in the grave any faster than I'm going."

"I just don't want you in an accident, Mama."

"How's that little *nieto* of mine?"

"He's fine, getting smarter every day. Today he told me his *abuela* was a smart cookie."

"He said that about me?" Lucinda laughed.

The following Sunday night when she went to the bingo game at the Sisters of the Precious Blood, that Romeo, Ramón Fernández, was waiting for her in the parking lot. Or maybe he was waiting for someone else. She had to crane her head over the steering wheel now that she'd shrunk some, and though she'd never tell her son, she preferred to arrive before dusk so she could see the white lines she needed to park between. Just that morning, she'd gotten another pesky letter from the homeowner's association. She promptly threw it away. Miguel may have convinced her to live there, but she didn't have to abide by all the silly rules.

As she pulled into a spot, she figured Ramón must be waiting for some *señora* who'd by now plied him with albondigas soup and homemade tamales, the sweet-smelling corn husks cooked to a perfect tenderness.

But he wasn't waiting for someone else.

"Señora Sánchez?" he said politely. He handed her a bouquet of herbs—coriander, chili pepper, cumin, epazote, and vanilla— a straw bow holding them together. Some of these weren't mentioned on her Board-approved plant list, and she missed them from North Park. The blues, golds, and reds and the spicy smells reminded her of her own mother's warm kitchen, cooking over the hearth.

"Oh, call me Lucinda, for heaven's sake," she told Ramón. She didn't have time left in her life for such formalities. Did he really want her to take these? Well, she wouldn't mind having them, but what did it mean?

"You have captured my heart," he said. He removed his straw hat, the same one he wore, she found out soon enough, when he gardened, to prevent skin lesions, though his skin was already a dark reddish-brown. He held the hat before his chest, like someone had died.

"For goodness sakes, what is it, Ramón? Let's get our seats before she starts calling." She could tell just by listening to him that he'd been born and raised in Mexico while she was from the United States. What could she and this man possibly have in common?

He swiveled his body so it faced the direction Lucinda was walking, but he didn't follow.

"You are a strong woman," he began. "You do not do what others wish. You wear comfortable, worn-out bedroom slippers to keep your feet warm, *calientitos*, and without blisters, and you do not care what others think. They are ugly slippers. I congratulate you."

Oh, brother.

When he wasn't looking, though, she admired his high cheekbones, his round sun of a face, his short, husky body.

"You carry your own liquor to keep yourself warm on the inside," he told her. "You do not put up false fronts so that people will like you for who you are not."

She managed to get him inside the mission, where she figured he'd stop babbling and the biddies would take him over. But he followed her straight to her spot underneath Jesus Christ Our Savior. He spent the entire evening sharing the flask of Southern Comfort she'd smuggled, tucked into the band where her hose were rolled to the knee. The man was corny as hell, and yet the language barrier forced him to be genuine. He didn't have the skills to be sarcastic or cruel.

Still, she went to a different bingo game the following weekend. She breathed easier, didn't worry about being watched. She could stay inside herself, think her own thoughts. She wore her lucky sweater, the one with the weave unraveling at the elbow, making her feel snuggled up, *a gusto*. She didn't even wear a bra. Who cared? She pushed a chair in front of her so she could keep her slippers perched high, good for her circulation and bunions.

But the following weekend she couldn't stop herself from returning to the Mission. Would he be there?

She'd become so distracted by Ramón the last few weeks—those eyes, the dark hair, the grin—she kept forgetting to water her lawn. Let her son water it if it made such a big difference to him. See how happy it made him she had to live here. After that first husband of hers, Emilio, nobody was ever going to tell her what to do again.

Damnit. *Híole!* The love years were supposed to be behind her. Did Ramón say the same thing to all the ladies at the bingo hall? The frail, the lonely, all of them having outlived the men who shared their lives? Was he looking for free burritos from a *señora* who would cook for him every night? Emilio had been good for one thing. When he finally kicked the bucket, his generous ship welder's pension had allowed her to quit all her years of waitressing, with the stipulation that she not remarry. She'd finally been able to relax.

But there was Ramón in the parking lot again that night. Not only did he watch her drive in, but when he saw it was her, he stepped up and directed her with big, dramatic gestures so she would have no trouble fitting between the white lines. Seeing him waiting for her made her stop caring so much about the lines in the first place. He presented her with a single dried rose, the petals fragile and elegantly shaped, the precious leaves still full and partly green.

"You are a real woman," he told her, in a way that made her both soften and bristle, like a cactus flower. She was doing just fine by herself.

"You have a large bosom that holds a great heart," he told her. "And your large bottom gives you no reason to worry that it will grow. You keep your hair gray so a man doesn't feel he has to keep up but can relax. I have bedroom slippers as well." Emilio had always made fun of her big butt, *grandes nalgas*.

She and Ramón shared Southern Comfort for the entire three hours of the bingo game. "I live in North Park," he whispered to her at one point. "You will love it there."

Half her body felt needy again—what made him think she would ever go to his home? The other half briefly relented—the mere mention of her old neighborhood, where she'd lived all those years, mellowed her.

"I used to live there," she told him. "Such a beautiful area."

"You must visit! I will drive you."

She curled her lip, but realized they could almost have gone to high school together. "I graduated from Sweetwater Union High. 1955," she told him.

"I went only briefly to school in Chiquimitio, in the middle of Michoacán. Then I moved to work in the fields of California. I still send money to my wife, who has two of my children, but I will never go back. I have not seen her or my children in . . ." His eyes watered up.

Lucinda's hand reached out to pat his knee, to comfort him, but all she could really think about was the fact that he was married. He'd abandoned a family. Was his hurting a woman's heart any better than Emilio's shoving and hitting her?

She stood from the game. "Don't talk to me anymore."

She stalked to the door, Ramón stepping on the back of her slippers he was so close.

"Señora Lucinda, please wait. What have I said?"

"You have a wife. I don't need more wounds."

"But," he said, as they traveled toward her car, "but I stayed away so long making money for my family she met another man. And then I fell in love with another woman. My wife and I no longer knew each other."

He was still talking through her rolled-up window when Lucinda drove off.

He showed up at her door on Monday. Had she given him her address? Maybe he'd seen her driver's license when she'd taken it out of her pocketbook to make a donation to the Sisters.

"Let me in, *señora!*" he called from a window.

"Leave me alone!" she said.

And finally he did, after a lot more knocking. But this didn't necessarily make her happy. If his wife had met a new man, was this Ramón's fault?

The next Sunday she returned to bingo. And Ramón was waiting. She'd planned to be aloof, but then she wasn't.

"I have saved and bought a weed whacker," Ramón said gently, clearly wanting to get his whole story out on the table, "a lawn mower and a blower. Now I work at the gringos' houses and did not spend a cent until I bought two condominiums in Poway and a small cottage in North Park. I repaired the places myself."

"North Park, eh?" she said longingly.

He would leave his money to his children who never knew

him, he told her. They'd been raised by a different man. He didn't
need Lucinda's money. He didn't want to marry any more than
she did. His only private garden now was on the deck he'd built
onto the cottage he lived in, the one in North Park. Lucinda lent
him her Kleenex. She touched his shoulder as he silently wept
about his children, while the sister in the severe black and white
habit continued calling out bingo numbers.

The first time she saw his place in North Park was at a
neighborhood block party given by one of his neighbors. She
loved the area. No home owner's rules here.

The party was on the thirtieth anniversary of the PSA flight
that had gone down in the late 70s. Like everyone else in San
Diego, she remembered exactly what she'd been doing when the
plane crashed at 9:00 that morning. After getting Emilio and
Miguel off to work and school, she'd been on her way to work
when she saw the black smoke bloat upward and then take over
the hills. A long time ago.

Even though some years had passed since Emilio had died,
she still worried about what witnessing his father's temper
had done to her son. True, it had been mostly her that Emilio
had taken his rage out on, but once or twice he'd hit Miguel,
too. Maybe that's why her son acted like a bully these days
when he raised his voice to get her to the doctor or to hire a
housekeeper.

That night after their bingo game and all the Southern Comfort,
Ramón called a cab to drive them home, to her home. She liked
the way he took charge while she waited on the curb. Lord knew
she could take care of herself, yet it was nice after so many years
to have someone who wanted to help. He slept on her sofa. She
covered him with the afghans she'd made after her retirement.
She couldn't see well enough to make them anymore, and besides,
her arthritis made her hands hurt.

"*Ay*," he murmured, practically purring with the comfort he
felt. "A woman's hands," he said, not seeing anything wrong with
hers. "A woman friend." Soon he was snoring like Emilio used to.

Only it didn't bother her when Ramón did it. She just hoped her son wouldn't stop by. He'd never approve.

The next night she made him homemade *sopes*. They were so exhausted from the cooking and the talking they fell asleep by 7:30 p.m. Together. In her bed. Not waking until 6:00 a.m. Who was there to care how long they slept? They'd earned the right.

Over the following month, they revealed their parents' love stories, confided family secrets, appraised Ramón's previous wife and her Emilio's metamorphosis from passionate suitor to agitated ogre.

"Come with me, *mamacita*," Ramón said when they'd finally said what they needed to say and decided to make love. That night he helped remove her shift, she his trousers. The dim light from the bathroom bathed their wise, desirous bodies. Ramón smoothed the skin on her neck for such a long time it felt like a shiny sea stone. She ran her nails over his back until he drooled.

"Don't fall asleep yet, *papacito*," she murmured.

Love that night wasn't about getting it over and pushing Emilio's dead weight aside before he dozed off. This wasn't to say that Lucinda and Ramón didn't fall asleep right in the middle of everything. But it was a pleasant sleep. A siesta. And when they awoke early the next morning, they picked up where they'd left off. Ramón actually cared where those folds between her legs led, what they could do, that Lucinda felt something too, that the episode wasn't over until she had produced a certain song in her chest.

"*Mi amor*," Ramón said afterward. A man of Ramón's age didn't have to finish any sooner than his woman wanted him to.

As the weeks and months of their new life together glided by, filled with lovely lovemaking, she needed more rest. That's when her lawn really started turning brown. Of course Ramón noticed it, gardener that he was. But Lucinda wouldn't allow him out in the yard. "These big building honchos can't tell an old lady what to do," she said. "Besides, Miguel will think he's won. I'll get to it." And then she sprinkled the flowers a little.

One morning Miguel made a surprise visit since she never picked up her phone anymore. "I'll get you an automatic sprinkler." Lucinda's complex hadn't had an automatic system when she moved in though most of her neighbors had now installed them. "I'll put it in when you're not here." Lucinda hadn't told him about Ramón who, fortunately, was at work when Miguel arrived.

"I don't need one! It's my house!"

"But, Mama! The Association keeps leaving me messages that I have to do something about your property. Remember, I signed on as the person to contact in case of an emergency!"

"They consider this an emergency?"

"You have to get the place in order, Mama. If you can't, I'll have to start looking into retirement homes for you. This is crazy." His voice rose, like the old days with Emilio.

"I don't care if you are my son, don't you talk to me like that. Get out!"

But then, just as Miguel was about to leave, one of the Association's private security officers parked in front of her house. Agitated, Miguel watched the man walk up. Lucinda noticed her son's hands stretch out reflexively, the fingers sharp and spread like rakes.

Miguel swung the door open and snatched the letter from the man, who never got the chance to knock. "Leave my mother alone!" he said, his chest thrown out like a peacock's, his long hair suddenly seeming like plumage. Lucinda watched her son's jaw jut, his chest square as he leaned closer to the man, and she didn't like it. Just how much Emilio was there in her son?

The following afternoon, Lucinda pulled into her driveway after doing her errands and made a mental note about how brown the grass was. As soon as she'd set the groceries down, she'd go back and at least sprinkle. But once inside she began thinking about the chiles rellenos and tortilla soup she planned to make Ramón for dinner. She did not have the lolling free afternoons anymore when she did nothing but watch *telenovelas,* not now that she was having an affair. They shared a companionable silence, nothing expected. Not that Ramón was perfect. The enormous work boots he left lying around the living room were like boulders she tripped over. He forgot to let the cat out, and she pooped in Lucinda's indoor ficus. He'd left a wife and two children behind in Michocán. But she was growing to love him.

Besides, she rationalized, San Diego was a desert. Almost all the water they had was piped in from Colorado. Why should she be ashamed of brown landscaping and the lawn in its natural state? San Diego was on voluntary water control. It was just the damn gated community that wanted to water the hell out of everything.

Miguel swung by again a few weeks later.

Thus far, Lucinda had been successful at arguing Ramón out on walks when she knew Miguel was coming. She still hadn't told her son anything. What man with the kind of machismo her son had grown up with wanted to know his eighty-year-old mother was having a love affair?

"I don't want to go on a walk, *novia*," Ramón said that morning, like he frequently did, when she saw her son pull up and then tried to coax her man out the back door. "This boy needs to know there's a man in his *madre's* life."

"But he's my son. After his Papa, he probably thinks all men will hurt me."

Ramón shook his head, but being from Michoacán, he no doubt understood tradition even better than she.

Would Miguel believe how much more pleasurable sex was now than when his mother was in her thirties with his father? More likely he'd think she'd been raped. No way would he understand that when you were as old as she and Ramón, there was nothing more to live up to. Those kids on the television were another species. Things didn't have to go in and out of other things if you didn't have the energy. How big or small or hard or soft or fast or deep wasn't the point anymore. You were lucky to find someone who still had a hankering. If she wanted oil down there, she had oil down there. She had always wanted oil down there, even when she was young, but Emilio had said there was something wrong with her if she wanted it. The difference was that with Ramón she could have anything she desired.

"Nothing much going on," she told her son.

"Why don't you ever answer when I call?"

"Too much energy to get to the phone, *mi'ijo.* Besides, I call you back later."

She should have left Emilio sooner, before her son saw so much anger. But she couldn't afford it on her waitress salary, and Emilio would never have given her a dime.

She and Ramón went to a different church on Sundays to keep things quiet.

"Are you embarrassed of me, *mi reina?*" he asked.

"Don't be a fool, Ramón. We need some peace." She didn't need the old biddies ogling them at church. She'd played by the rules all these years. She was entitled to a little pleasure.

By now her lawn was completely dead. Like straw, it crunched under their feet.

Sometimes Ramón convinced her to come down to his place and spend the weekend. "I'm not getting married," she said.

"No one's asking, *mamacita.*"

One time when she was visiting North Park, she finally met the couple around the corner, Alexa and Eduardo. Lucinda had heard that the couple had had a mystical experience down in Rosarito Beach and now they constantly kissed and held hands. And it was true, the whole time she and Ramón talked to them, they smiled and touched each other. Ramón said Eduardo no longer seemed to work—he'd quit right after their odd experience.

Then came the knock on the door one Monday morning at 8:30. Neither Lucinda nor Ramón was expecting anyone. She surveyed the living room, which had newspapers lying around, old glasses, like somebody lived here, not nearly as stark as when she had lived alone.

"You better go out the back door," she told Ramón.

"Why?" Ramón said.

"I have a bad feeling about Miguel coming by," she told him. "At least hide in the bathtub. Pull the shower curtain across."

"I'm not going to hide in the *baño*. I'm tired of hiding from your son."

"*Ay*, please, Ramón."

Ramón disappeared on her behalf, but she knew he didn't like it.

The same security guard the Homeowner's Association had sent a month ago stood on the front porch when she opened the door.

"Ms. Sánchez, are you aware your lawn is brown?" he asked.

"Yeah. Now that you mention it." She considered the lawn from the doorway, the sun shining down, and she was reminded of the pretty golden grasses on rolling hills that California was known for, though she doubted he was here to thank her.

"There's an ordinance in this community, ma'am, about maintaining your landscaping."

That damn son of hers. Who wanted someone keeping track of how you lived your life, what color you painted your house, whether you had a yard sale?

"I don't know who decides what's pretty and what isn't," Lucinda said, trying to stand still, though it was hard because her hip hurt from where she'd stretched the muscle in bed with Ramón the previous night. She needed to sit down.

"The HOA gave you a booklet of the bylaws when you moved in, Ms. Sánchez," the man said. "It's got all the CC&Rs clearly spelled out."

"The CC&Rs?"

"Covenants, conditions and restrictions."

"I'll decide how my yard looks." Lucinda began pushing the door closed.

"Ms. Sánchez," he said, writing on a pad. "The HOA has left repeated warnings."

He was holding out a citation for her to sign, and she was feeling dazed. That's when she got him. She didn't mean to, she just wanted the situation to go away so she could go lie down, and didn't think fast enough. Slammed the door on his hand. He howled. It all happened so fast.

"You bitch!" he shouted at her. "You're going to be sorry!"

She was more than sorry. After his engine started and his tires screamed around the corner, Lucinda herself screamed and ran to the back of the house. About her own violence, all the violence.

"What is it, my love?" Ramón asked, stepping over the fluffy pink bathroom rug.

Her anger at Emilio was suddenly coming out of her seams. Now she herself had caused bodily harm. She had to stop all of this.

"You stay there, Ramón. I don't want my son to see you. I don't want him to hurt you."

"I will not hide."

She would have to call Miguel. He'd say he'd warned her, but that didn't matter.

"*Mi hijo!*" she said into the phone. "You must come over here right away!"

"What's going on, Mom? What happened?"

"The Homeowner's Association! I crippled his hand!"

"What?" After a brief silence, he muttered, "I'm on my way, Ma."

When she turned around, Ramón was gone, invisible again.

A police car was at her house before there seemed time for it to get there. The security guard, poor man, she could see him from her front window standing by the curb, his figure slumped, his hand wrapped in a large ice bag.

A rap on the door.

"What is it?" she called.

"Ma'am, it's the police. You have to open the door. A man has been injured."

She opened it. A youngster in a uniform stood before her, a little acne still speckling his face left from high school. An equally young female partner behind him.

"I need to see some identification, ma'am," the boy said, his oxford shoe immediately braced against the door, "so we can write up the incident."

He looked almost sorry, but that didn't mean Lucinda wanted to be accosted in her own house. She feared she might say something rude and tried to slip further inside, to casually shut the door, but she couldn't help shaking when the officer stuck a baton in the way.

"Ms. Sánchez," his pony-tailed female partner said, "we don't want to arrest you for assault. If you'll just cooperate and talk to us, we can probably make this all go away."

"Assault?" She couldn't think straight.

"You hurt someone pretty badly. And the HOA has a citation for you—failure to maintain landscaping. They'd like to work something out with you."

She knew she should cooperate, but she'd cooperated too much in her life. A wrenching feeling swept through her that if she did everything they said, all this happiness she'd found so late in life might be taken from her. She wasn't going to allow some Emilio-like Association to step in and take away all her freedom.

Where was Miguel when she needed him? He'd be able to solve all this. It was a misunderstanding. And even if she'd made a mistake, her son couldn't force her to go to a retirement home. She had her rights.

Without thinking, she tried to push the door shut on the boy. She'd call Miguel again. He always wanted to control her life. This was his big chance.

"Ms. Sánchez, you can't hurt people like this," the cop said. He shook the foot she'd just absent-mindedly crushed in the door. She'd harmed another person. What was becoming of her?

The boy gently urged her out of the house and onto the front porch.

All this over browned grass? Who cared about a lawn when you were in love? she wanted to scream at them all.

Miguel pulled up, so upset he drove over the curb.

"What's going on here?" he said.

Didn't she deserve this last part of her life to be happy, without so many troubles?

"Who are you, sir?" the boy cop demanded.

"I'm her son. And I want to know what's going on here."

"She hurt a security officer pretty bad," the cop said.

"Mama?"

Lucinda, befuddled, looked at her son and was reminded that he'd always been a good boy. She'd never had to discipline him. And she'd never pressed charges against his father when he'd caused her bruises, even cuts. She liked to think she would now.

She sank to the top step while Miguel talked to the policemen.

"Mama? Who is this man?" he said, suddenly.

She turned, peering through her front door, and saw Ramón marching down the hall toward them, an angry look on his face, shoulders rigid.

Immediately, Miguel told the police, "This strange man does not belong in my mother's home. Do something!"

The policewoman stood in Ramón's path to prevent a confrontation.

"Ma'am, do you know this man?" she asked Lucinda.

Ramón spoke first. "Excuse me, officer, but why are you standing in my way?"

Despite his forthright tone, the look of fear on Ramón's face caused part of Lucinda's insides to crinkle up and die. No matter how long he'd been in the States, no matter that he owned his own business and property, his language difficulties still made him feel like an outsider, and she knew this.

"We don't know this man," Miguel told them.

"Ramón!" Lucinda said, standing and reaching for him.

"Ramón?" Miguel repeated.

"*Mi esposo!*" Lucinda was excited now and snapped out of it.

"Mama, you don't have a husband."

"In all but certificates, that's who he is, son."

Miguel glared at Ramón as if he'd performed some unspeakable atrocity on his mother. "My mother's getting senile," he told the officer.

The stocky Ramón burst around the officer's stance and stood chest to chest with Miguel, whose face had gone red. Ramón said, "Do not ever talk of your mother this way again or I will see to it that you are very sorry!"

Dios mio! Lucinda watched gratefully as the officers pulled her son and lover apart.

The security officer whose hand she'd slammed appeared as tired of the whole thing as she was. Suddenly the cop car in which he was a passenger roared off.

The young cop said, "So, ma'am, you're okay with this man being in your house?"

"Yes."

"I live here!" Ramón said.

Miguel turned to the officer. "But . . ."

The couple quickly grasped each other and held on.

"But . . ." Miguel gave Ramón the stink eye. "We need to talk about this, Mom."

"*Reina*," Ramón said, kissing the inside of Lucinda's arm.

"Miguel," Lucinda replied, knowing that a simple explanation would never calm her hot-headed son, "if you don't leave right now, I'll never speak to you again."

"Keep an eye on her, son," the officer said as he and Miguel walked out to their cars.

As the days went by, then weeks, Miguel visited more, not less. At least Lucinda finally decided to pay a little more attention to watering the lawn, which wasn't exactly green, but was no longer brown either. So what did her son complain about instead the first time he came over? "What happened to the housekeeper we agreed on?"

"I let her go months ago," Lucinda told him.

He turned away.

Ramón, sitting beside her on the couch, said gently, "It is your *madre's* home, and she will make the decisions, no?"

"You're not my father," Miguel said, slamming the door on his way out.

The next weekend, though, when he returned, he found the old man on the back patio and handed him a *cerveza*. "Didn't mean anything by it," he said grudgingly. "Just want to protect Ma."

Ramón raised the beer in good will. "You love your mama."

Not long after, Lucinda was preparing fish tacos and flan for Miguel, his favorite meal.

Ramón told her, "You can't afford to buy all these ingredients, *mamacita*. And what about all this time on your feet? You must take care of yourself, not let him dictate you."

"You don't seem to mind when I'm making something for you," she said.

"It is not good to have him over here so much. He's hard on you."

"I'll have my son over whenever I like."

"*Ay*," Ramón said. Flustered, he left the room.

There were days Lucinda wanted to ban both of them from the house for a moment of tranquility. The problem was she loved them.

Sometimes Miguel seemed happier phoning her than visiting so he could speak freely, without Ramón, though often enough Ramón sat beside her when she took her son's calls. But when Miguel called two weeks after she'd made his favorite dinner, Ramón was having trouble with his bowels and had spent most of the morning on the toilet with a deteriorating tube of Preparation H. Lucinda had the opposite problem and took Metamucil. Who needed young whippersnappers around who didn't understand these things? What did they know of intimacy?

"I want to see my grandson," Lucinda told her son that day, as she often did.

When she could get Miguel to bring little Oscar over, she shined. Only someone older could see the absolute beauty of youth, the innocence. And he loved his *abuela*. The boy was so playful, took pleasure from so little—bouncing balls, creating forts out of handwoven blankets, digging in the dirt outside. Of course, Ramón could have interested him more in the garden, but when Miguel came over, he kept his body between his son and Ramón.

Miguel shoved through the door one day, not even bothering

to knock. Furious. Bringing Oscar along as a witness to this foul
mood. Lucinda had never seen him so bad.

"I talked to his past employer, *Madre*," he hissed, "the tomato
grower this Ramón used to work for." His voice, even at a whisper,
made the windows rattle. Little Oscar stood still, frightened. "He's
married, *Madre*. The man is married. He has other wives."

Lucinda stood. Ramón was off in the bathroom again with his
problems.

Stomping into the kitchen, Miguel seemed to be trying to spread
his foulness. Oscar jumped as his father's work boots grated against
the linoleum.

"Don't you talk like that in front of your son," Lucinda said.

Miguel glanced quickly at Oscar. "Go outside and play, *mijo*."
Oscar was only too grateful to run away into the yard.

"He has only one other wife," Lucinda said, "but he hasn't
seen her in years. And you forget, I'm not married to Ramón."

"But don't you care that he's married? What's become of you,
Mama?"

And there, right as he said it, he found sitting on the counter
for all the world to see a plastic bottle of personal lubricant. It
was from the day before, when Lucinda and Ramón had made
love against the dishwasher, before Ramón's knee went out.

"That's it!" Miguel said, now throwing himself around, actually
looking for Ramón.

"Miguel!" Lucinda shrieked. "Stop it right now! He's not well."

But Miguel couldn't turn himself off that quickly.

"Why, Mama?" Miguel looked down the hall of Lucinda's little
house. "It's disgusting!"

"Because I wanted to! I've been having sex since long before
you were born."

"Where is he?"

"You get out of here!" she shouted at him. "I'm calling the
police if you even touch him. It's not like the old days when your
father could hit anyone he liked. And you leave that son of yours
here. I don't want him anywhere near you when you're like this!"

Just then Ramón rounded the corner to the kitchen, coming out of the bathroom again, panting, exhausted, to see what all the noise was. Miguel was so revved up he had no control. He hit the old man right in the gut. Ramón fell to the floor like a sack of flour. The old man pulled his knees to his chest, a snail trying desperately to recede into his shell, only the shell was as fragile as he was.

Shocked, Miguel peered down at the kitchen floor. "Papa!" he said. It was like he'd hit his own father, who now lay out on the floor. Like unfinished business.

Still, Miguel managed to shout at Lucinda: "I forbid you to have this man in the house ever again!"

They lounged on the front porch of Ramón's cottage, his hand gingerly rubbing the inside of Lucinda's thigh where he had left a love bite during their romancing the night before. "I am sorry, *mi vida*," he said. "Was I too passionate?"

"You're never too passionate, Ramón." She leaned over and softly kissed the side of his neck, something she'd never done to Emilio or anybody else in her life.

Ramón had finally retired several months earlier and sold the two rental condos. Lucinda sold the damn house with all the damn gated neighbors concerned about the color of the damn lawn. He'd had no trouble sweet-talking her into living in his old cottage, his favorite abode in what was still her favorite neighborhood, North Park. Even though she'd lived there with Emilio, she wasn't going to let him ruin it. It was *her* place. And it didn't take long to get to know more of the neighbors.

Her son had been banned from her home while Ramón recovered from his swelling and contusions. Lucinda had made good on her threat and called the police; she had to finally stand up against the violence. The cops had taken her son to jail, but only booked him overnight while things cooled off. She and Ramón didn't press charges.

At first Miguel was so hurt his own mother had called the

cops on him, he wouldn't allow her to see her grandson. Eventually, he gave Ramón a gruff apology, but was vehement about keeping his son at home. Even his wife could do nothing about it. Lucinda pined for the little boy, Oscar, and during darker moments she hoped she hadn't made a different kind of mistake since now she wasn't able to keep an eye on the child at all.

"You have to let me see my baby," she told Miguel.

"Soon, Mama."

The Sisters of the Precious Blood pretended not to have heard the story at all, and when Lucinda and Ramón played bingo on Sunday evenings, she positioned her photo of Oscar so it looked over Ramón's cards, too. They sat in their usual spot, under Jesus Christ Their Savior.

After a few months, Miguel began dropping Oscar off at Lucinda's new home, letting the boy run inside to visit, though Miguel himself refused to leave his car. "Don't be thinking it's because I'm happy he's coming here," he said, turning his face away to avoid laughing at his mother's crooked smile when she stuck her head through the passenger-side window.

Lucinda wanted to wrap her arms around his son's neck in gratitude, for not being Emilio after all, though he'd lost his temper. But she let him get over his machismo in private.

Now that Lucinda lived with Ramón in North Park, the neighbor ladies seemed to like to congregate on her patio. Macaws flew in and made themselves at home as well. A scarlet and a greenwinged liked to sit beside each other on the clothesline, lightly swinging. Heather came by, having now broken up with her UPS man, saying she needed to grow up and learn a few things on her own. Lucinda heartily agreed as she served the girl *limonada* from the back tree one afternoon. Heather had now taken up ceramics, the sound of the foot pedal on her used wheel ricocheting through driveways and patios from above. The poor girl around the corner, Annie, finally lost her husband to AIDS. Lucinda encouraged her to lay on the chaise lounge while Lucinda hung laundry nearby to dry in the sea breeze. They talked. At least Wes and Lauren seemed to have moved permanently back into the neighborhood from Hemet, a good thing since Annie and Lauren had become even closer. Even Sabrina came by, and the two of them complained about the sons they didn't get to see enough.

Some of the prettiest plants Lucinda and Ramón now owned were those he nurtured on the cottage's deck, the drought-resistant ones: the agave, the aloe vera, the birds of paradise—nice ripe colors of green and orange.

Sometimes when she and Ramón took their neighborhood walks in the evening, they stopped, hushed, when they reached the site of the plane crash, and Ramón would leave a bouquet of zinnias at the stop sign. Words were suddenly unavailable when standing at such a bleak crossroad. All those people.

But mostly North Park brought Lucinda peace. If Ramón's home had had an association with an ordinance about what people could or couldn't place on the grounds outside, there'd no doubt have been complaints about the two worn-out easy chairs Lucinda and Ramón liked to sit on out front—plaid and too big to completely fit on the porch. But there weren't any ordinances, and so often they fell asleep out there with the sun shining on them.

A Note from the Author

My deepest gratitude to all who have contributed to *What Happened Here* over the years by reading drafts, offering a place to write, or by supporting my writing. These stories started presenting themselves to me many years ago, between, during, and after other writings. I know I'm going to forget to thank some people. Feel better knowing that the minute I remember I didn't acknowledge you, I'll appreciate you all over again and feel horribly guilt-ridden.

You rock, Steve Almond, for being my mentor, for believing in me, for helping me to shape these stories the way I wanted to write them, only better, for giving time you don't have, and for caring.

I am grateful to the National Endowment of the Arts for awarding me a fellowship that meant I could take time off work to write and for believing in me when I was in a particularly low moment of writing self-esteem.

My gratitude to The Virginia Center for the Creative Arts, Dorland Mountain Arts Colony, Ragdale, Yaddo, and MacDowell, and for the support and the gift of time and space in my busy life to write these. I hope you know how much you mean to all of us. And thank you to The Tin House Summer Writer's Workshop, where I've hung out for many summers getting invaluable criticism and writerly support.

The San Diego Community College District and my school, Mesa College—including my friends and colleagues on campus and my students—have been behind me from the beginning and offered multitudinous manners of support. I'm thankful.

I am forever indebted to Kevin Morgan Watson for making my dreams come true. I wanted so much for *What Happened Here* to be published by the awesome Press 53. You kept in touch with me about the book for years, offering guidance and then great sensitivity and help once you accepted the book. Christine Norris, I appreciate all your insight and edits.

I love your "Red Bird" on my cover, Sandra Tweed!

To my dear friends, Christine Ladewig, Scott Starbuck, and Pianta, who support my writing and everything else I do. What would I do without you?

Muchas gracias, Sylvia ZoBell, Mary ZoBell, and Claude ZoBell for help with the Spanish.

For readings of the book, sometimes multiple times, bless you, Marko Fong, Lucinda Nelson Dhavan, Cliff Garstang, Mary Akers, Myra Sherman, Heather Fowler, Jim Ruland, T. J. Forrester, and Jerry Gabriel. I've had my lucky share of valuable writing groups over the years, the members of which also read these stories more than once. I so appreciate your friendship and criticism, Lana Witt, Judy Reeves, Gerri Brooks, Michelle Zive, Patty Santana, Nina Roselle, Judy Geraci, Scott Barbour, Judy Geraci, Josh Goldfaden, Rava Villon, Paula Marguiles, and Gail Chehab.

Zoetrope Virtual Studios is a wonderful haven where I've met so many talented writers who've helped me grow immensely—I love all of you. I can't possibly name everyone here but, in reverse alphabetical order naturally, thank you Bryan Shawn Wang, Townsend Walker, Donna Vitucci, Nathaniel Tower, Marie Shield, Ellen Parker, Shane Oshetski, Richard Osgood, Stefanie Nellen, Sam Nam, Sequoia Nagamatsu, Cynthia Litz, Lucinda Kempe, Robert Kaye, Len Joy, Patti Jazanoski, Debbie Ann Ice, Jeanne Holtzman, Kyle Hemmings, Jim Harrington, Alicia Gifford, Barry Friesen, Stefanie Freele, Kathy Fish, Diana Ferraro, Anne Elliott, McKenna Donovan, Katrina Denza, Gay Degani, Myfanwy Collins, Louis E. Catron, Doug Campbell, Rusty Barnes, and so many more of you.

BONNIE ZOBELL lives in a casita in San Diego with her husband, dogs, cats, and many succulents. She is the author of *The Whack-Job Girls*, which came out in 2013 with Monkey Puzzle Press, and a recipient of an NEA Fellowship, a PEN Syndicated Fiction Award, the Capricorn Novel Award, a spot on Wigleaf's Top 50, and she had a notable story included in storySouth's Million Writers Award. Her fiction has appeared or is forthcoming in such magazines as *The Potomac Review, Connotation Press, The Los Angeles Review, PANK,* and *The Greensboro Review,* and she has been a fellow at Yaddo, MacDowell, VCCA, Dorland Mountain Arts Colony, The Wurlitzer Foundation, and Villa Montalvo. ZoBell received an MFA from Columbia University. Currently she teaches at San Diego Mesa College, is an Associate Editor at *The Northville Review* and at *Flash Fiction Chronicle,* and is working on a novel. Her website is www.bonniezobell.com.